DEDICATION

For All Those Who Kick Ass, Take Names
and Read Books

ANGELBOUND TALES VOLUME ONE

BOOK ONE OF THE ANGELBOUND TALES SERIES

CHRISTINA BAUER

COPYRIGHT

Monster House Books

Brighton, MA 02135

ISBN 9781956114669

First Edition

CONTENTS

FOUR. HERBIE AND BABY
HOTDOGS

FIVE. SAVING MRS.
POMPLEMOUSSE

ALSO BY CHRISTINA BAUER

APPENDIX

AUTHOR NOTE

Note From the Author, Christina Bauer

*D*ear reader,

Welcome to *Angelbound Tales Volume One,* a collection of five bonus stories from the world of Myla Lewis, including:

One. Walker's Love Connection

Two. Sharkie and Snickerdoodles

Three. Wedding Bells

Four. Herbie and Baby Hotdogs

Five. Saving Mrs. Pomplemousse

Originally released in special editions, these many tales now unite in one master collection that spans print, ebook and audio formats!

Warning

If you don't like quirky indie authors, then you'll hate the following disclaimer from my inner pirate:

Shiver me tinders, if ye haven't read Angelbound books one through three, then these tales'll frustrate ye more'n a drunk goat on astroturf. Argh!

Now back to my regular pirate-free self:

I hope these stories provide a little escape from reality because, let's face it, we all need one.

CB

ONE. WALKER'S LOVE CONNECTION

Introduction From the Author, Christina Bauer

Dear reader,

This tale takes place *before* the events of Angelbound book one. In it, Myla sneaks into Purgatory's Arena where she discovers a romantic secret about her honorary older brother, Walker.

I hope you enjoy the story of *Walker's Love Connection*!

Sincerely,

CB

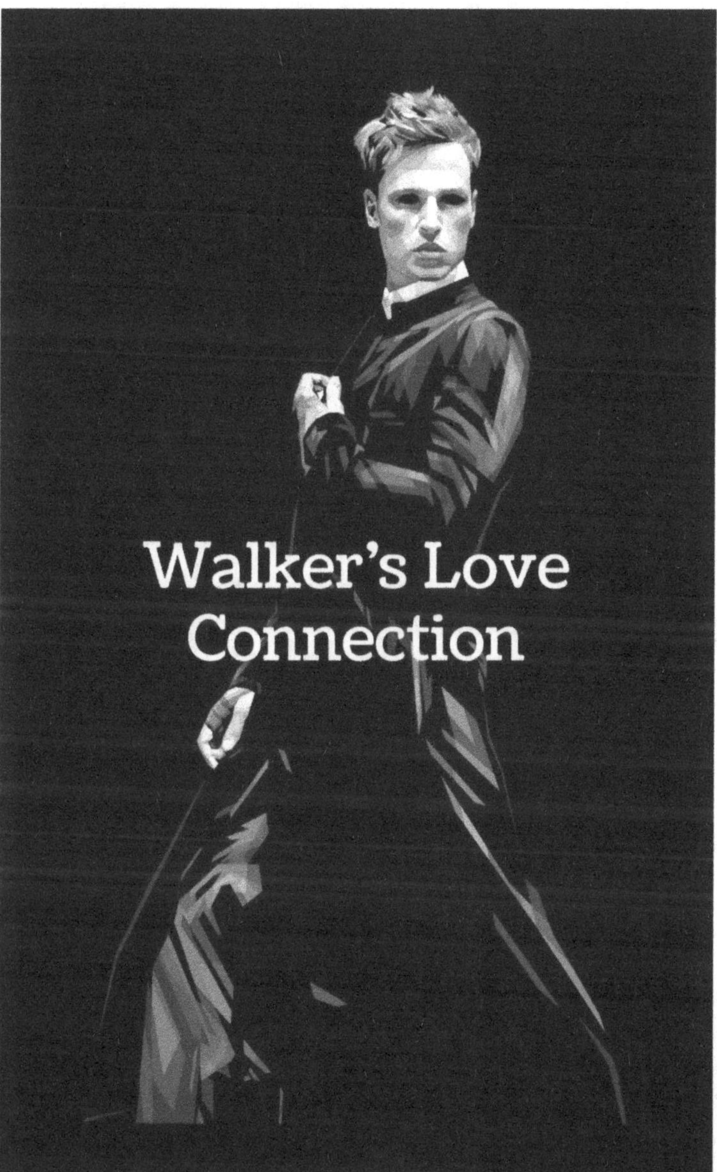

Walker's Love Connection

1

My tail and I *always* get along.

Until we don't.

Take now, for instance. I drive my ancient station wagon, Betsy, through the many strip malls and weedy lots that make up Purgatory. My ride is an un-pimped junker whose radio stays eternally stuck on a polka station. As 'Roll out the Barrel' blares from Betsy's tinny speakers, my tail jabs my shoulder in time to the music. This is its way of saying, *I'm not happy with our destination.*

My tail loathes trips to the Ghoul-E-Mart.

"Come on," I plead. "I promised Mom to pick up milk from the Ghoul-E." Technically, our overlords sell us something called *white liquid product.*

Saying that I'm only getting milk makes zero difference to my tail. Right now, it's the star of its own little play called, Poke Myla's Shoulder.

Jab, jab.

"We aren't going to the Ghoul-E right away," I explain. "We'll hit the arena first."

There's only one arena in Purgatory—it's where warriors like me fight evil souls and demons to the death. Is this an appropriate extra-curricular activity for a high school junior? Ah, no. But, that's ghouls for you. Our overlords see their minions—meaning quasi demons like me—as the equivalent of pond scum.

My tail pauses for a moment as it considers a potential arena visit. Then, it acts in a way that says, *what a load of B-S.*

Jab, jab, jab.

Clearly, my tail has trust issues. It doesn't believe we're going anywhere near the arena. And there are two reasons why I shouldn't approach the gladiator games right now. First, it's not my day to fight. Second, even when I *am* scheduled to go, I should only show up with my honorary older brother, a ghoul named Walker.

But I have plans, people.

I turn onto a mostly-empty lot behind a tall ruin made of gray stone. *Purgatory's Arena.* I steer my wagon into a parking spot that's hidden by tall grass.

"We're here," I announce.

My tail gives me one last jab. Little by little, the arrowhead-shaped end turns to scan beyond my shoulder.

And it goes nuts.

For a full minute, my tail bobs up and down with such joy, it slams between the wagon's roof and its pleather front seat. I can't help but smile. While my tail hates Ghoul-E-Mart, the arena is another story.

Suddenly, my tail freezes mid-happy dance. The arrowhead-shaped end points right at my nose. This is its way of saying, *you can't go in there!*

"We're just watching a few matches. It's exhibition day." This is when other quasi fighters hit the arena floor to show their skills against demons. I'm here to size up the competition.

My tail's arrowhead end points at my watch before swaying from side-to-side in a *no-no-no* motion. In other words? *This isn't your day to fight.*

"Please," I comment. "Who'll pick me out from the crowd?"

With a graceful whoosh of motion, my tail forms a straight line across my dashboard before tilting its arrowhead end up at a ninety-degree angle. It then shifts back and forth in its very best impression of a certain water-bound predator.

A shark.

Translation: *The emcee for arena battles is none other than your nemesis, Sharkie the ghoul. He'll notice you, Myla.*

Even worse, if Sharkie catches me sneaking around, I could end up in a ghoul re-education camp, and that's if I'm lucky. Fortunately, I have a plan.

I pull out a mangy paper sack from under the passenger seat. "See this?"

My tail bobs up and down. *Yeah.*

Opening the bag, I pull out some supplies for this mission, namely a blonde wig, floppy hat, and oversized sunglasses.

I slip on my new disguise and check the windshield mirror. A long blonde wig covers my red tresses. Heavy sunglasses conceal my brown eyes. A wide hat tops off the look. Sure, I still wear grey sweats and matching sneakers, but the ghouls make everyone wear that.

With this disguise? I am no longer Myla Lewis, demon killer. Now, I'm a blonde bombshell with excellent taste in both eyewear and headgear.

I focus on my tail. "Be honest. Do you recognize me?"

My tail makes a great show of scanning me from head to toe.

"Well?" I prompt.

Looping around, my tail points to itself. The meaning is clear. *You look okay. What about me?*

"Exactly. You need a disguise, too." Reaching into the bag once more, I pull out a pair of googly eyes and pop them onto my tail's arrowhead end. "Boom. Now you're a googly snake."

Is that a real animal? *No.* Will anyone notice? *Hey, if they buy my wig, hat, and sunglasses, then a googly snake will be an easy sell.*

My tail rises to check its reflection in the driver's-side mirror. It must like what it sees, considering how it points to the door. *Time to go.*

In some back corner of my brain, I realize this is one of my dumber schemes. In all honestly, I probably will get caught.

But before that? Oh, what joys await me.

I grasp the car door handle. *Trouble, here I come.*

2

I cross the parking lot, careful to flip my long golden locks over my shoulder as I go. I figure that move is very blonde-bombshell-y, so my disguise seems all the more believable.

The fighter's entrance is around back. After a short walk through some tall weeds, I reach a crumbling stone archway. The guard on duty is a she-ghoul named SAS-3. I call her Sassy, because she really has a mouth on her. I respect that in any life form.

Sassy leans against the stretch of wall beside the entrance arch. Like all ghouls, she wears long black robes, only Sassy's have a leather waistband with a holder for her cattle prod. Although her hood is drawn low, Sassy's all-black eyes gleam as her gaze locks onto me.

Here's what should happen next. Sassy will ask me a bunch of questions to verify my identity. I've a whole story ready, too: I'm a prospective fighter who's here for today's expo match. I even came up with a new name for myself, Jolie Warhammer. I open my mouth, ready to tell everything.

Sassy shrugs. "Proceed."

"Really?"

"Sure, Myla. Walker's already arrived."

I'd worry about why my honorary older brother is here without me, but Walker's sneaky like that.

"You don't want to ask anything else?"

"Nah, just go in," says Sassy. "The sooner you're out of my sight, the faster you're Walker's problem, not mine."

See what I mean? *Total smart ass.*

I shift my weight from foot to foot and consider my options. This situation is both good and bad. The nice part is that I'm getting past Sassy with such ease. The crap side is how my disguise clearly sucks. And if Walker's in the arena already? That could complicate things.

Still, Sassy's job is to recognize people as they walk into the fighter's entrance. On this side of the building, there's nothing else to do but watch weeds grow. If anything, it's good luck that Sassy's waving me through without trouble.

I march under the access archway and through a series of stone tunnels. The arena itself is a great oval. Concentric stone benches encircle the fighting floor. I take care to enter the stands at the oval's short end, aka the opposite direction of where Sharkie always faces the crowd.

Heh heh heh. This is so awesome, I can't stand myself.

After parking my butt on an obliging stone bench, I scan the arena itself. The fighting floor is empty. Small groups of ghouls sit on the benches opposite mine. All these undeadlies wear black robes with the letters QFG on their hoods. They're the Quasi Fighting Guild. The QFG reports any quasi fatalities. For some reason, it takes five clusters of undeadlies to do this.

Ghouls. They love their bureaucracy.

Suddenly, a figure appears in one of the nearby archways that lead out onto the arena floor: an extra-tall ghoul with leathery skin, beady all-black eyes and teeth that have been filed to sharp points. My pulse speeds.

That's Sharkie, all right.

The emcee strides onto the arena floor. This is what I consider to be the risky part of my plan. If Sharkie glances toward his left, he'll spot me, easy peasy. I slump lower on my bench-seat and hope Sharkie will walk faster.

He doesn't. Sharkie slowly lurches along. The

emcee's black robes are especially ragged, so they billow with every step. At last, Sharkie reaches the floor's center. He slams his long staff onto the ground.

"I have an announcement," calls Sharkie in his gravelly voice.

I sit up straight again. Even my tail gets into the act by pointing its new googly eyes toward the arena floor. Adrenaline kicks through my system. What will the first demon be? Battle slug? Octo-fiend? The possibilities are endless.

Another familiar form steps out from a nearby archway. Although it's a ghoul with their hood drawn low, I know the identity of this mystery ghoul. After all, there's only one person who pulls off that particular combination of confident stride and ass-kicker boots.

My honorary older brother, Walker.

Walker approaches Sharkie. They whisper together for a while before Sharkie re-addresses the audience. "It seems we are out of quasi sacrifices for the day." Sharkie glares at Walker. "Although I know there are more if we really look."

"We need to end the games," says Walker. It might be my imagination, but I think Walker shoots a sideways glance in my direction. It would be such a *Walker move* to ruin my fun.

"And so we shall," says Sharkie in a low voice. "But not before one last match."

Walker shoots another worried glance in my direction. "We're out of fighters. You haven't called the match to start. You can't have a battle now."

"In that case, I call for a performance of the Up With Quasis troop!" Sharkie slams his staff onto the ground.

I hiss in a disgusted breath. Up With Quasis are kids my age who do dance routines between matches. I don't get the appeal, but a lot of folks like them. Their biggest hit is a song called 'I Love Sub-sub-subjugation." It's as humiliating as it sounds.

I expect Walker to shrug and walk away. That's not what happens. "We don't have to do that," says Walker. And I may be imagining things, but his voice might wobble a little bit as he speaks.

"Principal Inertain, bring your students here!" As Sharkie speaks these words, his eyes glow with demon light. Ghouls communicate telepathically. No doubt, Sharkie is using his skills to summon the Up With Quasis to the arena. They used to be a quasi-led performance arts high school. Now, they're run by a ghoulette named Principal Inertian.

Sure enough, a tall rectangle appears by one of the access archways. A bunch of quasi high schoolers march out from the portal and hang just inside an access tunnel.

My shoulders slump with disappointment. I guess the Up With Quasis kids have to practice, too. Still, I was really hoping to size up my competition. Mostly because I like winning.

Soon, one of the access arches is filled with the Up With Quasis kids. I wonder if they really like singing 'I Love Sub-sub-subjugation' or if they find sneaky ways of being a pain in the ass. Like me.

The portal vanishes. A ghoul appears under the access archway, Principal Inertian. Her hood is pulled low, but I know it's her. Every other ghoul wears long black robes. Inertian's the only one who has shortened her robes into a dress and added black go go boots.

Inertian doesn't seem interested in organizing her kids. Instead, she keeps scanning the now-empty arena floor. It doesn't seem like there will be any matches today. And I still need *white liquid product* from Ghoul-E-Mart.

Another ghoul steps out from the inner shadows of the access hallway in order to chat with Principal Inertian.

It's Walker. Huh. So, that's where he portaled off to.

You know those cartoons where little hearts appear around someone's head? The way Principal Inertian gazes upon Walker, she could have those hovering over her hood right now.

I can only see Walker's back, but his head is bobbing in short and decisive movements. I've seen that before. Walker's laying down the law.

In reply, Inertian grabs Walker's forearm. Even from this distance, I can see how her lower lip quivers. Walker breaks free from her grasp and steps off into the shadows once more.

I purse my lips and consider this turn of events. Walker is a total vault when it comes to talking about his life outside of keeping my sweet ass out of trouble. I didn't know he had friends, let alone she-ghouls who yank on his sleeves for sketchy reasons.

Color me curious. I am totally bringing this up the next time I see Walker.

Which is right now, as it turns out.

Walker steps out from the same access archway that I used a few minutes ago to reach my seat. My honorary older brother looks at me and shakes his head.

I'm so shnagged. It's a hella big rule for me not to visit the arena on my own. I suspected Walker spotted me before. But now, I'm definitely in trouble.

Walker steps along the empty row, heading right for me.

I steel my shoulders, waiting for the big speech about

how I'm forbidden from sneaking off to the arena without him. Walker plunks down beside me. "Myla."

"Walker." I raise my pointer finger. "Before you launch into your lecture, there are a few things I need to explain."

My honorary older brother says seven words that blow my mind.

"I need you to pretend we're together." He shoots a nervous glance toward the access archway and 'Up With Quasis' performers. Sure enough, Principal Inertian is glaring hot death at me and Walker.

Whoa.

*M*y tail arches up to point at my nose. It's as shocked as I am. "I know," I tell my tail. "This is huge."

Walker sighs. "Myla."

"My name for today is Jolie Warhammer."

"MYLA."

Normally, Walker is Mister Cool. Not today. He arches his body toward me while shielding his face with his hand. When Walker next speaks, his voice is a nervous whisper. "Did you hear what I said?"

At this point, I could just answer him. *Yes, I heard you.* Or, I could ask for details about Walker's love life. Yet, an even better idea appears.

Walker and Mom have always been in a *secret cabal* about yours truly. Namely, they're totally hiding the truth about my dad's identity. Sure, it could be neat to know what Walker does in his downtime. Yet, the more I think about it, the more I'd rather know who I should send a card to on Father's Day.

And this moment. Here. Now. I could get Walker to tell me everything. I just need to soften him up first.

So, I gesture casually toward my tail. "No comment on the googly eyes? You never miss stuff like this."

"Myla, please." Walker's looking at me with his big black eyes all extra wide. I really am a sucker for that face.

"Yeeeeees?"

"Don't try to work this. I won't tell you anything about your father."

Sure, I get that my disguise isn't the best. But how could Walker know I planned to ask for info about my father? My honorary older brother must be using a divining spell.

I raise my pointer finger again. "Excuse me, I can tell that you're using—"

"There's no magic involved here," interrupts Walker. "You're always asking about your mystery dad."

My tail now nods at me with a motion that says, *Yes, Walker's right.*

I glare at the arrowhead end. "Traitor."

"Please, Myla. Will you help me or not?"

At this point, Walker's really working his big watery eyes. I crumble like an old cookie.

"Okay," I state. "What do you need?"

Walker exhales. "Take off your hat."

I pull off the floppy headgear. Along the way, I almost yank free my wig. Walker grabs handfuls of hair on either side of my head to keep everything in place.

Down on the arena floor, Principal Inertian keeps staring at me and Walker. Those little hearts over her head could now be tiny daggers. "Hat is off," I report. "Now what?"

"We lean our foreheads together while you block our faces with the hat."

"Everyone will think we're smooching."

"No, Inertian will think I'm kissing… whoever it is you're dressed up as today."

"My secret identity is Jolie Warhammer." Still, I shift my massive hat so I hide our faces from the rest of the arena. Then, Walker and I lean in until our foreheads are almost-not-quite touching.

Talk about awkward.

"How long do we have to do this?" I ask.

"Forty-three more seconds ought to do it. Then, she'll give up."

"Will you tell me anything about the situation with Inertian?"

"What do you wish to know?"

I do a double-take. "I didn't think that would work. You never share anything personal."

"Better ask quickly," says Walker. "This is a limited-time offer."

"Okay." Suddenly, the awkwardness vanishes against the chance for secret Walker info. "Did you and Inertian date?"

"Define *date*."

I purse my lips. "This is way out of my wheelhouse. What other options are there besides dating?"

Walker winks. "Time's up." He leans back on the bench, resting his arms onto the stone lip behind him.

I narrow my eyes. There's some secret code in all this dating language. I'll ask my best friend, Cissy, about it later.

Walker looks out over the arena floor. "Cissy will know," he states. "Unless you really want me to tell you now."

"I'll take the *now thing*."

"Inertian and I hooked up."

"A one-night stand. Okay, I get it." I scrunch up my face. "Aaaaaaaand that's more than I wanted to know."

"Which is why I gave you a choice."

Out on the arena floor, Sharkie slams his staff onto

the ground again. "And now I bring you, 'Up With Quasis!'"

Music strikes up from tinny speakers. The Up With Quasis kids sashay out onto the arena floor. They barely get through the first line of 'I Love Being Sub-sub-subjugated' before Inertian speeds out into the middle of the group.

"Stop!" she cries. "Take that again from the top. All of you are making bad choices. It's time to move on from this song and start another, better song. And we'll run that tune over and over until you get it right."

When I next speak, I take care to whisper from one side of my mouth. "She's talking about you."

"I'm afraid so."

"This is starting to feel even more awkward."

"Oh, it's not so bad. Imagine the moment your mother discovers you snuck into the arena." Walker shoots me the side eye. "I don't mind you watching expo games at the arena, but you can't go alone."

On the dance floor, the quasis start up a new song, 'MacArthur Park With Worm Soufflé.'

An idea appears. "I'll make you a deal."

"Hmm?"

"If we leave right now, I'll never breathe a word to anyone about Inertian and you won't tell Mom how I snuck in here."

"You have a bargain."

As Walker and I march back toward Betsy, I think about the absolute perfection that is my life. All I care about is fighting. There are no one night stands with random show choir ghouls to interrupt my battle obsession.

As if in agreement to my inner thoughts, my tail rubs its googly-eyed end across my cheek. With any luck, it will just be me, my tail and our arena fights, forever.

Once again, that little voice pipes up in the back of my head, reminding me that with my luck? I probably will meet someone one day. I turn the idea over before dismissing it completely.

Yeah, right.

Chuckling, I load back into Betsy and focus on something far more important. *What's the fastest path to Ghoul-E-Mart?*

~

—The End—

The adventure continues in our next story, Sharkie and Snickerdoodles!

TWO. SHARKIE AND SNICKERDOODLES

AN ANNIVERSARY BONUS STORY

Introduction From the Author, Christina Bauer

Dear reader,

This tale takes place *before* the events of the Angel-bound book one. In this story, Myla seeks out frosted snickerdoodles from a bakery that's also 'home sweet home' for Sharkie, Myla's old nemesis from Purgatory's Arena.

I hope you enjoy *Sharkie and Snickerdoodles*!

Sincerely,

CB

Sharkie and Snickerdoodles

oo ne noo. Noo ne noo. Nothing to see here.

I sashay along a cracked sidewalk. The sky threatens rain, which is typical for Purgatory. All around me, empty storefronts look out over the deserted street. My destination for today is a little place around the corner. My mouth waters as I consider the yum that awaits me.

La Ghoule Bakery, aka the only spot in Purgatory that sells freshly-made frosted snickerdoodles.

And today, I shall get those snickerdoodles in my tummy.

I'm not supposed to be anywhere near this bakery— long story--so I'm wearing a disguise. Pausing before one of the many darkened windows, I check out my reflection. My red hair is hidden under a long blonde wig and floppy hat. My brown eyes are concealed by massive sunglasses. Even my tail is in costume. Namely, I've attached a pair of googly eyes to my tail's arrowhead-shaped end.

The rest of my outfit is gray sweats with a matching T-shirt and raggedy sneakers, which is the standard outfit required for all quasi demons. All in all, I look great.

My tail shivers, a movement that makes its googly eyes roll around. My tail happens to have a mind of its own. Shivering is a dead giveaway.

"You're worried."

My tail bobs up and down. *Yes.*

"Hey, I get why you're riding the anxious train to worry town. The chick who runs La Ghoule Bakery happens to have a live-in boyfriend that isn't totally cool." I make my eek face as I say the words, *totally cool.*

In reply, my tail tilts its arrowhead-shaped end up ninety degrees and slides back and forth in a pretty good imitation of a certain aquatic predator.

"Yes, the baker's boyfriend is Sharkie."

I fight evil souls in Purgatory's arena. Sharkie is both a ghoul and the emcee for these death matches. We have a healthy hate-hate relationship.

"But as you can see, we're both disguised."

My tail loops the arrowhead end around my ear. *You're nuts.*

"It's not the greatest disguise, but it's good enough for Sharkie. Probably." My stomach growls. "Hey, a growing girl has needs."

My tail flops down to hide behind my ankle. Clearly, it still isn't convinced we're safe. But me being me, there's a particular piece of info that I've been saving up just in case my tail got cold feet. Not that it has legs, but you get the idea.

"Hey, there's another reason not to worry. We're here at the ass-crack of dawn for a reason. The bakery opens up early today so they can be inspected by a ghoul delegation. No one knows about this. There won't be any lines. We'll be in and out so fast, Sharkie won't have time to react."

My tail slinks out from behind my ankle to point at my nose. *How do you know this?*

"Walker told me." I make little quotation marks with my fingers when I say the words *told me*. "Rather, Walker didn't tell me anything. It's more that I snuck a look at some papers in his satchel." My tail tilts its arrowhead end, which means I'm making progress. "So, you're okay with visiting La Ghoule Bakery, right?"

The arrowhead end bobs up and down. *Yes.*

"Perfect."

I resume my march around the corner and make a beeline for the only nice-looking building in the neighborhood. The La Ghoule Bakery has two bay windows which flank a thin wooden door. I pause outside.

Dark-cloaked figures lurk inside the shop. It's the visiting delegation of ghouls, just as Walker predicted. The only other person inside is the renowned Madame La Ghoule herself. My heart pitter-pats at double speed as I realize the truth.

There's no sign of Sharkie.

My stomach growls again. I rub my tummy. *Soon, my friend.*

*a*fter years of imagining, I'm about to realize my dream: *frosted snickerdoodles from none other than Madame La Ghoule.*

I stride inside the bakery. Along the left wall, there stands a shoulder-high glass case of baked yumminess. This display ends in a waist-high combination of counter and register. Tinny speakers play French accordion music. The scent of freshly-baked cookies fills the air.

Grrr. My stomach growls yet again.

I inch closer to the display cases. Sadly, the ghoul delegation blocks my view into the snickerdoodle section. Even worse, these undeadlies are taking for-bleeding-ever to finish their inspection.

A ghoul I've decided to call Tall Guy reads from a

sheet of paper in his undead hands. "Let's continue. Again, I read form A-972-B, the weekly update report from ghoul manufacturing in Purgatory. Next question, 162-J." Tall Guy clears his throat. "Are éclair sold at this store?"

Madame La Ghoule is a round she-ghoul who wears a white apron over her black robes. She straightens her white chef hat before replying. "Oui."

"Why is there an accent mark on the word éclair?"

"Zat eez how zee word is spelled."

"Are you sure éclair needs an accent mark?"

"Oui."

I want tell Tall Guy to move on already, but I'm trying to be in disguise here. So, I bite my lips shut instead.

Tall Guy sighs and turns to the other ghouls. "I can't decide. Do you think we should we list it with and without an accent, so no one is confused?"

This conversation sucks up ten minutes, minimum. It's taking everything in me not to scream.

After they decide to spell éclair two ways on the form, the group finally moves on to other, equally useless, questions. Madame La Ghoule patiently answers each one.

At last, someone in the delegation declares, "We'll talk about this and come back later."

Classic move of ghoul bureaucracy.

The group slowly trudges out the door. Finally, it's just me, Madame La Ghoule, and the snickerdoodles. As I move closer to the display case, I know that an angelic choir doesn't really break into a version of Handel's Messiah, but it sure sounds like it in my head.

Treat of treats!

And snack of snacks!

For I shall eat this snickerdoodle

Snickerrrrrrr-dooooooo-dolllllllllllle!

I blink a few times and look around. Madame La Ghoule stares at me with an unreadable look.

Oops. I may have gotten out of myself a little there.

I shift my weight from foot to foot. "Uh, I was just..." *And that's all I got.*

"Allow me to guess," says Madame La Ghoule in her cute French accent. "You were hearing a version of Handel's Messiah in your head, only the lyrics were about snickerdoodles?"

"Yes, how did you know?"

She shrugs. "For some reason, that happens to all my snickerdoodle customers."

At this point, it's important to note that ghouls who spent their human existence in France are a little different from other undeadlies. Namely, they won't eat worm soufflé or any of the other standard ghoul meals.

Yes, that makes them way cooler than the average ghoul.

Madame La Ghoule steps closer to the display case. "My customers are the ghouloisie. I only let certain quasis buy from me… as in, ones I know are not scum." She narrows her eyes at me. Obviously, I'm not on the pre-approved guest list.

Now, there's a lot to dislike about what Madame La Ghoule just said. Being called scum may sound nicer in a French accent, but it's still mean. As a rule, I sass off in situations like this one. But for snickerdoodles? I'll make an exception.

"What do you want to know about me?" I ask. "I'm an open book." Even if I am wearing a wig, floppy hat and sunglasses.

"What kind of tail is that? Tell me the truth."

"It's a googly snake."

"I did not know such a beast existed."

"Well, it absolutely does. Duh." And a little bite comes through my tone. I can't make that much of an exception.

Madame La Ghoule nods. At last, she asks the question of my dreams. "What would you like to order?"

"A dozen frosted snickerdoodles."

"What flavor?"

This is a shock of the very best kind. "What do you have?"

"Ah, I make zee Amaretto, Apple, Anise, Apricot…"

Clunk.

For the first time, I notice a door set in the left-hand wall. Someone beyond that threshold is making a ton of noise.

Madame La Ghoule calls out toward the door. "Silence, mon cher!"

My stomach sinks. I'm pretty sure who the *mon cher* is in this situation. *Sharkie.* Time to move things along.

Madame La Ghoule focuses on me again. "Avocado, Acai…"

I hold up my hand. "How many more flavors are there?"

"I'm just on the a's."

"You know what? If you've got chocolate, then that's my order."

"Twelve snickerdoodles with frosting *du chocolat*, good choice. Now, what kind of casing do you want?"

Here's the issue. I've never actually gotten into this bakery before, let alone placed an order. Normally, Sharkie's around, so I couldn't risk it. All of which means the casing situation is a new one.

"Casing? What's that?"

Madame La Ghoule takes out a sheet of golden tissue

paper. "I make zee little origami shapes around each treat. It only takes a few minutes for each one. You can have swan, unicorn, parrot, owl, shark…"

"You know what? You can skip the casing."

"But I make zee little origami shapes."

"Buuuuuuuut all I want is a dozen snickerdoodles."

When Madame La Ghoule next speaks, her irises light up with demon power. "For quasis, I always make zee little origami shapes. You appreciate the effort and pay more, oui?"

"You price gouge quasis for origami?"

"I. Make. Zee. Little. Origami. Shapes."

In other words, there's no way I'm getting out of here without an origami casing on every freaking snickerdoodle.

Clunk, clunk! More noises sound from behind the door.

"Mon cher! Are you all right?"

A familiar gritty voice echoes in from behind the door. "Yes."

If I'd jammed my tail into an electrical socket, I could not feel more of a charge. *That speaker is Sharkie, all right.*

"I'll be out in one minute," growls Sharkie.

Madame La Ghoule turns to me. "Zee poor man." She gives me a look that invites me to commiserate.

"You don't say." *As in, don't say this. Please.*

"He works in zee arena. You wouldn't believe zee trouble a nasty girl fighter gives him. She is foul. Evil. Zee worst quasi scum."

I should ignore all that and get my cookies. However, life's not all about baked goods. Only *mostly*. Plus, this is an unprecedented opportunity for Sharkie-related gossip. "Really? How much does she bug him?"

Madame La Ghoule sighs. "Oh la la. He comes home so upset."

"Huh. How much?"

"He goes into zee bathroom for hours."

"Does he cry in there? Tell me he balls so hard, there are snot strings involved."

"Non, in zee bathroom, he files his teeth to razor-sharp points, all the better to tear out Myla's throat the moment he ever gets the chance!"

More clunking sounds echo in from beyond the door. A weight of worry settles on my shoulders. *I'm really pushing things here.*

"You know what? I'll take one chocolate snicker-doodle in a swan casing, please." I accent this order with a big smile. *One snickerdoodle is better than none.*

"Ah, that will only take me a few minutes." Madame La Ghoule pulls out a sheet of golden paper with an exaggerated flourish. Crinkles sound as she futzes around with the casing. No further noises come from the Sharkie part of the building.

At this point, I'm feeling good about bad self. First, I get into the bakery, no problem. Second, I order a frosted snickerdoodle. Third, I avoid Sharkie. And fourth, I'm now about to escape without incident.

I can't really see what Madame La Ghoule is up to behind the display case. Still, it seems to take for-bleeding-ever for her to finish. At last, she throws up her hands and smiles. Madame La Ghoule sets the wrapped snickerdoodle into another bag and holds it high.

I rush over to the cash register part of the store. "Ready to pay!"

Madame La Ghoule calls toward the door again. "Mon Cher! I need your help with zee register!"

"You know, there's no point bothering *mon cher*." Reaching into my pocket, I pull out a handful of bills and dump them on the counter. It's a ridiculous amount for one snickerdoodle. "Keep the change."

Madame La Ghoule spies the cash. She steps closer. My mouth waters. One more step and Madame La Ghoule will be close enough that I can take the bag and run.

Suddenly, the back door slams open. None other than Sharkie marches into the space behind the counter.

He's a lanky ghoul in his tattered black robes. His skin is gray and leathery.

Madame La Ghoule sighs. "Mon cher, it's you at last."

Sharkie winks. "I'll take care of the cash register."

Madame La Ghoule still holds my bag. Only now, she's taken a decided step closer to Sharkie. In other words, my snickerdoodle remains well out of reach.

My tail shimmies beside me, which is its way of laughing. It gestures toward the exit. The meaning is clear. *Want to go?*

I shake my head. *No way am I giving up now.*

What happens next moves so slowly, it's like we're all underwater. Little by little, Sharkie reaches his bony arm forward until he snatches the snickerdoodle bag from Madame La Ghoule. His head slowly swivels to face me. He grins, showing off his mouth of pointy teeth.

A pang of rage zings inside me. This is the ghoul who's sent me into countless battles, trying to kill me. Sure, I always win, but still, there's a point here. Sharkie's goal was to destroy yours truly. And now, this ghoul is all that stands between me and my freaking cookie.

Sharkie holds the bag high. "What did you order?"

I speak in a high voice, just to throw him off. "One snickerdoodle."

What happens next is a nightmare. Sharkie opens the bag and basically shoves his undead face in there. He snorts while inhaling deeply. "Is this chocolate?"

"Correctimundo." That's really old shtick, so I hope it acts as verbal camouflage.

Sharkie looks between me and the register a few times. Since this is Purgatory, the register is one of those old iron numbers that I could use as a projectile if necessary.

Hey, when you're me, you have to plan for all contingencies.

"You remind me of someone," says Sharkie, still in his underwater-slow mode.

I try to keep my voice high and perky. "Did you see all the money I piled up by the register? Hand me the bag and you can keep the change."

"If I cared about money, why would I volunteer here?" asks Sharkie.

I do a double take. "You volunteer?"

"Yes. I'm paid in… *special snickerdoodles*." Sharkie looks over at Madame La Ghoule as he says the words, *special snickerdoodles*. A sick taste seeps into my mouth.

Oh, Hells. Now I have to wonder what that weirdness means.

"Thanks for sharing," I say brightly.

"You're not… afraid of me?" asks Sharkie.

Madame La Ghoule raises her hand. "I'm sooooo scared of you, mon cher, in case you're wondering."

Eew. Just eew.

Instead of responding to Madame La Ghoule, Sharkie lumbers closer. "I meant you, quasi. You should be frightened. You're about to beg me to spare you, isn't that right? Admit it, and I will give you the cookie."

That crap crosses a line. Something snaps inside me. Even a snickerdoodle isn't worth this.

"Nooooooo," I say slowly. "I want you to hand over my freaking snickerdoodle. Now."

Sharkie leaps over the countertop to land before me. Let the record show that this move exposes his skinny chicken legs. This whole trip is turning out into way more than I ever bargained for.

Sharkie yanks off my wig and hat combo. The sunglasses fall off on their own, the traitors.

"Ha!" A manic gleam shines in Sharkie's black marble eyes. "It is you, Myla Lewis! "

"False! Look at my tail." I gesture toward the appendage in question, which still sports its disguise. "That's a googly snake!"

Fortunately for me, Sharkie can be sharp as a box of rocks sometimes. *Like now.*

"Oh." Sharkie scans my tail. "My bad."

All this time, Madame La Ghoule has been hanging

in the background. Now, she rushes toward the register and fishes through the pile of cash. "I'll finish the transaction. Apologies for any confusion."

My tail arcs up to point at my nose. I know what it's thinking. *We shouldn't degrade ourselves any further for a snickerdoodle.*

How wrong my tail is.

I smile sweetly at Madame La Ghoule. "Thank you so much."

And here's where my tail becomes a pain in my ass. It slams against the floor with such force, the googly eyes fall right off.

I groan. *So close.*

Sharkie points at the now-exposed arrowhead end. "Ah, ha! I knew it!"

I hold up my hands, palms forward. "That's my snickerdoodle. Hand it over and there won't be any trouble."

Sharkie clacks his pointy teeth together. "Run away or I'll bite out your throat."

I smack my lips. "Sure, you will."

Sharkie jumps at me, the dumbass. Leaping up into the air, I curl my legs by my chest and then pump my sneakers right into Sharkie's face. A satisfying crunch sounds.

Sharkie falls backward, unconscious. His ghoul robes

fall in disarray. Turns out, he wears boxer underwear with little red hearts on it. *More stuff that I didn't need to know.*

Madame La Ghoule wags her finger at me. "You're the one. The girl from the arena who taunts him. You call him Sammy."

"It's Sharkie."

"I'll call the ghoul correction squad after you!"

I gesture toward the still-unconscious Sharkie. "How about you skip the ghoul correction squad but take the extra cash?"

Madame La Ghoule narrows her eyes. "I accept zees offer."

I've been in enough fights to know one thing. Madame La Ghoule is totally lying.

"If you keep your promise, I'll never tell anyone about the Valentine's Day themed boxers."

Madame La Ghoule purses her lips. "Deal."

One thing about being a fighter: You learn when to retreat. And the joy of having kicked Sharkie in the face is so intense, I really can't imagine how this particular moment could get any better. With my chin held high, I march out the door and into my station wagon. I'm two blocks away when I realize the sad truth.

I pound the steering wheel. "Damn! I didn't get the snickerdoodle!"

My tail arcs up to show me something beautiful: It speared the snickerdoodle bag onto its arrowhead end. I yip with joy and pull over to the nearest curb. Tearing the bag open, I peel off the little swan origami thing.

At last, it goes into my mouth where it belongs.

And it really is the best. Melty chocolate. Sweet cookie base with a hint of ginger and cinnamon. Madame La Ghoule is a nut job to date Sharkie, but she bakes a fine snack.

It's all over in a matter of seconds. My tail moves to point right at my nose while shivering ever so slightly. It's ticked off.

"I get it," I state. "I should have listened to you at the end there. No snickerdoodle is worth groveling to Sharkie."

My tail bobs up and down. *Yes.*

"Although, honestly? Maybe that snickerdoodle was a *little* worth it." My tail freezes. "I'm not serious. And should I mention again that you were right? Well, you were totally right."

In reply, my tail bobs happily with the arrowhead end angled in a way that begs for a certain response. So, I give it a high five before driving away. Three more blocks pass before I realize something important.

I just downed my first frosted snickerdoodle and kicked Sharkie's ass, all within an hour of each other.

That's what you call a good day.

—*The End*—

The adventure continues in our third story, Wedding Bells!

THREE. WEDDING BELLS

Introduction From the Author, Christina Bauer

Dear reader,

This tale takes place *after* the events of Angelbound book one. In this story, Myla has just saved Purgatory and rescued her father. Now, her parents are getting married ... which should be a simple time, only when it comes to our heroine, stuff always get complicated.

Please know this story contains spoilers for Angelbound book one.

I hope you enjoy the story of *Wedding Bells*!
Sincerely,
CB

Xavier and
Camilla's Wedding

1

Three weeks ago, I defeated Armageddon. Go me. Yet ever since that uplifting kickassery, there's been an unexpected downside: hella boring dreams. As in, I spend all night eating kale. Looking for a lost shoe. Or even watching myself sleep.

Makes me want to poke out my dream-eyes with a fork.

But that's not what's happening tonight. Nope. Right now, my dream-self stands on the command deck of a starship.

Amazing, right? It gets better.

This isn't just any space vessel, mind you, but the star cruiser Xenolith from my favorite human television show, Stellar One. In my dream, everything around me is crafted in silver and white. A dozen crew members stand poker-straight before long consoles. All of them wear matching silver onesies because that's just how it works in space. And in the captain's chair sits *the* Commander Starling. I spent my entire sophomore year obsessed with his battle tactics. Outside of TV-land, Starling is a human actor named Foster Reins.

Well, he *used to be* human.

A few years back, Foster choked on a tuna sandwich, died, and became a ghoul. But in my dreams, Foster is still one hundred percent alive—as in tall and pale with a swoosh of dark hair over his wide blue eyes.

Long story short, this is a good dream.

A massive viewport covers one wall of the command deck. Starling gestures in that direction.

"Track Havoc activity," he orders.

My dream-self claps. The Havoc are badass aliens. They aren't demons, but not everything can be perfect.

The viewport flares to life, showing squat mini-humanoids in red luminescent armor. The Havoc. Which brings up a classic question for Stellar One fans: Why wear armor that makes you glow crimson? It's totally unhelpful when trying to stay not-dead in battle. For the record, I'm one of the fans who says, *relax, it's a TV show.*

"Cease displaying the Havoc," calls Starling. The viewport turns dark once more. My shoulders slump.

Too bad the Havoc fun is over. That said, Starling's next command makes up for the lack of glowing aliens.

"Show me Myla Lewis!" he cries.

My dream-self grins. *Suh-weet. Me time.*

The viewport brightens again. This time, it shows me in my Scala robes at the Great Summit, aka the big meet-up after I kicked Armageddon's ass. My goal for this event? Return Purgatory to self-rule. The view screen shows a scene from the meeting-a-thon in the Ryder ballroom. At this point, it's just me, the Ghoul Oligarchy, and *go time.* All during the summit, those four undeadlies tried to kill self-rule for my people.

This little chat is no exception.

"We cannot leave Purgatory," hiss the Oligarchy in unison. "Quasis are not ready to govern themselves."

Viewscreen Me huffs out a breath. "Only because you ordered your minions to hide all the files and stuff."

True fact: We don't yet have computers here in Purgatory, so this is a huge deal.

"Honestly," I continue. "I sleep for a few days after fighting the King of Hell and what do you guys do? Lock up all the bureaucratic everything. Not okay." I also suspect they've left some crap around to screw with my Scala powers, but one thing at a time.

"Many quasis have begged us to stay," counter the Oligarchy. "We only wish to heed their requests."

I fold my arms over my chest. "We've been over this, guys. Soon the quasis will vote on referendum Q8-29. My people can then decide whether to restart our old republic—"

"With your mother as president," interrupt the Oligarchy. (They totally hate Mom, by the way. Mostly it's because she won't put up with their crap. What can I say? It runs in the family.)

"No kidding," I counter. "She's the only one who wants the job." The rest of Purgatory's too scared of the Oligarchy. Not that I'll admit that part out loud.

"Your people may also vote to maintain their ghoul overlords."

"It's possible," I allow.

In one fluid movement, the Oligarchy lift their bony chins. "See? Even you agree."

"I did *not* agree." I raise my pointer finger. "What I said is that it's *possible*. Don't bet on it, though."

Outside the ballroom, voices raise in the hallway. Everyone's waiting for the Oligarchy's word on the referendum. Even *The Eternal Times* is out there. Sadly, if we don't get this vote scheduled, it may never happen. For the last twenty years, my people have been taught to do whatever the ghouls order. We quasis must start thinking for ourselves, pronto. This referendum is key.

Moving in tandem, the Oligarchy shake their heads. I

suppress a shiver. It's so creepy when they do stuff in unison. "We must respect the true wishes of the quasi people," declare the Oligarchy. "We refuse to allow the vote."

Which they can. Mostly because they hid all the voting machines.

Anger shoots through my limbs. On reflex, my tail arcs over my shoulder. *Battle mode.* For days, I've been holding back from going nuclear on these clowns. After all, I'm a demi-goddess now. I must act more mature. But it's been a long week of talking in circles.

Welcome to superpower time.

"Listen to me carefully," I say in a low voice. "We'll open these doors and announce that the vote will happen. Otherwise, Armageddon gets a one-way ticket out of Hell."

Key fact: I'll never release Armageddon, but the Oligarchy don't know that.

Lifting my arm, I summon a few dozen igni to materialize around my hand. For a moment, nothing happens. Then I hear the muted voices of my igni singing. It's music only I can hear, and it means they're coming to the rescue. A moment later, small bolts of power dive and swirl about my palm.

The Oligarchy gasp in unison. I won't lie; that's pretty satisfying.

When I next speak, I make sure that my eyes flare demon red. "I have had it with you guys. If you weasel out of this vote, I will release Armageddon, zip up to Heaven, hang out on a cloud, and leave you down here to manage the resulting shit-show on your own. The King of Hell hates you guys. As in loooooooooathes. He'll roast you for all eternity while I watch the barbeque." I deepen my voice to what I like to call, *lethal level*. "Just try me."

The four ghouls share a long look before slowly bowing their heads. "In that case, we agree to the referendum."

I've heard this before. "And where are the voting machines?"

"Hidden in the tunnels under Purgatory's Arena."

I purse my lips. *That's a really good hiding place, actually.* "Good. Let's go chat up the press." And then I'll find my buddy Walker and have him reclaim those voting machines. Walker's awesome like that.

Back in my dream, I stare at the viewport and sigh. Single-handedly forcing the Oligarchy to support the vote was fun. Dragging over a space-age swivel chair, I plunk my dream-butt down. If I had some demon bars and a remote, this could be sophomore year of high school again. Hitching my right leg over the chair's arm, I lean back and wait for more me-related ghoul ass-kicking to appear onscreen. That's not what happens. Instead the viewport blinks out. Everything darkens. A chorus of strange voices reverberate across the command deck.

"Great Scala," says one. "Come out!"

"Bless my kitten," adds another.

"Show us your igni," cries a third.

Crap on a cracker. These voices are not part of the Stellar One show. Sadly, my daytime reality is shoving its enormous ass into my dream life. *Grr.* A moment later, the command deck vanishes. I'm back in my mangy bedroom, tangled in my covers. Sitting up, I peep through my curtains to scan behind my one-story ranch house. In the misty pre-dawn light, my back lawn lies covered with a sea of strangers. Young. Old. All different kinds of skin colors and tail types.

My worshippers. Still here. Ugh.

I scan the crowd. There's an old dude with a cane, top hat, and a salamander's tail. A little kid with freckles who jumps in a mud puddle. I even spy an old lady in a purple tracksuit. Everyone stands a few yards from my window. I frown.

That's not right.

Where are my guards, anyway? I can't see much through the break in the curtain. Even so, there's no sign of the thrax warriors that Lincoln sends to protect me.

Normally, my guards stand about five yards away from the house, constantly enforcing a little policy I like to call, *no lookie no touchie.*

A moment later, a wrinkled face pops into my line of vision. It's the old lady in the tracksuit. "Great Scala, there you are. I need you to sign my armpit." Her voice carries easily into my room. No surprise, there. The walls of my house are paper-thin.

My mouth falls open with surprise. "You need what?"

"Your signature on my armpit," she says slowly. "So I can get the letters tattooed."

This is too much. I almost don't want to know the answer, yet I can't help but ask. "And why would you do that?"

"The tattoos will siphon off your powers. Then I can fly around, superhero-style."

"Huh." *And that's all I can say.*

Ever since I became the Great Scala, a shit-ton of crazy beliefs have sprouted up overnight. People think I can heal their pets or predict the future. Not to mention all the new businesses. There's a fresh cosmetics line called *The Myla Look.* Plus, there's the *Scala Girl* brand of clothing, shoes, hair products and snack foods. I don't get any money out of it—that's how things work in Purgatory. *Whatever.* The only time I get involved is when I fake-sponsor something crappy, like the *Myla Loves Ghouls* calendar. I killed that thing, fast.

But empowering quasis to fly via armpit tattoos? That's a shocker.

All of a sudden, the tracksuit lady steps away. Her face becomes replaced by one of Lincoln's guards, Harvey, a doughy guy with a round face, button nose and big ears. He's also a sweetheart and total goofball, which is why he's my fave.

"Sorry about that," says Harvey. "She got past us." No question who *she* is in this scenario: tracksuit grandma.

"What happened?" I ask.

"We saw what looked like a fire demon."

Memories from my dreams appear. "Wait. Was it a little round being in glowing red armor?"

"Yes. How did you know?"

"That's a quasi kid who's dressed up as one of the Havoc, aka the meanie aliens from Stellar One."

Harvey frowns. "Stellar what?"

"It's only the biggest human television show in the history of ever."

"Television." Harvey nods slowly. "I've seen those technology boxes while on demon patrol." He tilts his head. A mischievous gleam shines in his mismatched eyes. "Are you in danger?"

And here is why Harvey's my fav. His question is

actually code for, *do you want me to call Lincoln?* It's been way too long since I saw my guy, so I nod. "I'm in total and serious danger." Most guards would never push the rules for me, but Harvey's a softie.

Reaching into the pocket of his body armor, Harvey pulls out a purple paperclip and snaps it in two. A pouf of violet smoke balloons into the air above his palm. That's because Harvey wasn't really holding a paperclip. Nope. That thing is a thrax magic charm, and seeing those in action never gets old. In this case, Harvey's charm alerts a messenger to hit Antrum and find my guy. Nice.

Harvey clicks his heels and bows slightly. "Back to duty."

"See ya, Harvey."

Fresh voices sound from inside my house. This time it's Mom, and does she ever sound pissed.

"How dare he?" calls my mother.

Yipes. That's not Mom's "you'll be late for school" level of worry. Something is seriously wrong. Pulling off my covers, I slip on a robe and head for the kitchen.

This ought to be good. Or, considering how my life typically goes, epically bad.

rush into our kitchen. Like the rest of this house, the room is a little rundown. There are still punch-holes in the cabinets from when I played 'let's kill demons' when I was five. The floor tiles are so scuffed, you can't tell what color they originally were. Plus, the appliances are ancient and the ceiling's dotted with questionable patches of mold. You get the idea.

My parents stand around a small black and white television that sits on the scratched Formica counter. Everyone says Mom looks like an older version of me, what with her curves, red hair and long black tail. Sizing her up this morning, I totally agree. Dad's still recovering after his nightmare of imprisonment in Hell, so he's little more than skin and bones. At least, he's taken to putting on one of his classic grey suits in the morning. I take that as a good sign.

Mom and Dad don't look up as I approach. Their attention is still locked on the little TV. It's the kind with a bulbous screen and wire bunny ears sticking out the top. Believe it or not, this is pretty cutting edge tech for Purgatory.

Mom pokes at the screen. "Who does he think he is?"

In reply, Dad rests his hand gently on Mom's shoulder. He's not really chatty yet. Not that I blame him.

I step close enough to get a good look at the screen. What I see makes my mouth fall open in shock.

"That's Commander Starling," I announce.

"Commander who?" asks Mom. "There's no military left in Purgatory. It's one of the things we need to rebuild."

I take on my patient voice, the one I use when telling Mom the basics of modern life (like how hoop skirts aren't in style.) "He's not really a commander. Starling is a character on a human television series called Stellar One. It's one of the few shows we get in Purgatory."

Mom narrows her eyes. "And it's popular?"

"Huge. Everyone watches Stellar One. Remember sophomore year, when I joined his fan club?" Technically, I was named a Junior Commander level 2 in the

Lower Purgatory Division of the Commander Starling Fan Club. Not that Mom needs that level of detail.

Mom nods slowly. "I remember that. You quit."

Which is true. "I thought it would be more battle tactics and less drooling over Foster Reins."

Now Dad gets interested. "Foster Reins?"

"He's the human actor who played Commander Starling. Then he choked on a tuna sandwich and became a ghoul. No one really knows what he's been up to, outside of the annual Stellar One Convention."

Mom returns her attention to the small TV. "Well, he's causing trouble now."

On the small set, there appears a grainy black and white image from *Good Morning, Purgatory.* The host is a ghoul named GK-4. He's an older dude with a wrinkly face topped by a nest of gray hair. During his mortal life, GK-4 was a philosopher from ancient Athens. As a ghoul, he's turned his hooded robes into a sort of black toga. Everyone calls him the Greek. Believe it or not, he's one of our better media ghouls.

On the program, the Greek leans back in his chair. This set is one of those fake living room deals that are classic for talk shows. "Let me ensure I understand this," says the Greek. "As Themistocles stated, you cannot fiddle, but you can make a great state from a small city."

"Not sure what that means," says Foster with a

toothy grin. The guy looks like he did in life, except for the part where he's now super tall, more pale, and has all-black eyes. Foster still wears his Captain's onesie, which is a good choice. Ghoul robes are just blah. "But if that means I'm running for President of Purgatory, then you're absolutely right."

I pause.

Gulp.

Do a double take.

"Did he just say what I thought he said?" I ask.

"Oh, yes," replies Mom.

Dad eyes me carefully. "Do you think he'll give your mother any competition?"

"Oh, sure. You should have seen Foster in episode 32. He faced down the entire Havoc army. Took them down, single handed."

"That's just a television show," says Mom. "Foster didn't do that in real life."

"And that's my point." I tap my chest. "I fight demons on a regular basis, and even I have a fluid relationship with reality when it comes to Foster Reins. He's just…" I throw up my hands. When it comes to Commander Starling, there really are no more words.

Back on TV, Foster turns to the camera. "Vote for me on Referendum Q8-29 on Monday. Polls show that 87% of quasis already love my work as Commander Starling.

Now I'll steer this realm into the future as well." He raises his right arm, palm facing upwards, and stares off into the distance. It's the classic way he launches every mission. "Embrace the encounter. Live the Adventure. Follow me."

Too late, I realize that I said those last words out loud and in a dreamy voice. *Oops.* At least, the show goes to commercial break. No more chances to speak in unison with Mom's new nemesis.

My mother sighs. "Oh, Myla. If you're acting this way about Foster—" She lets the thought hang out there.

I lift my hands palms forward, surrender-style. "I'm totally voting for you next month."

"The vote is less than a week away," sighs Mom. "As in Monday."

"Oh, right." I could really kick myself now, but I don't have to. Instead, my tail arcs over my head and gives me a nuggie. "I get it, boy." I turn to Mom. "Sorry about getting all gooey over Foster."

"It's fine, honey." My mother sighs. "I'd rather you tell me the truth. This way, I know what the real threat is."

Dad points to the screen. "They're back from commercial."

On screen, the Greek addresses the camera. "We're

here with Foster Reins, the unemployed actor who's trying to make a comeback as President."

"Hey, I'm a working actor." Foster straightens in his chair. "In fact, I'm the main attraction at the annual Stellar One Conference."

The Greek ignores that statement and just keeps going. "And now, we return to our *Good Morning, Purgatory* exclusive. Foster Reins just announced he's running for President." The Greek turns to Foster. "What about Camilla Lewis? She's the mother of the Great Scala and the last remaining Senator. Do you really think you can beat her?"

Foster shrugs. "Well, she's not married."

I wag my finger at the TV set. "So what?"

There's a totally good reason my parents aren't yet married. Dad got dragged off to Hell right after my parents first hooked up. Mom's always considered him her husband. *Sheesh.*

The Greek rubs his jowls. "Well, Camilla had her reasons, isn't that right?" One thing I'll say about the Greek: When it comes to social rules, he's more laid-back than most ghouls.

"Only one thing is important," says Foster. "Camilla is finally marrying Xavier this Friday."

I gasp. No one is supposed to know about my parents and their secret wedding. Mom and Dad plan to visit Heaven on Friday morning for a small, private ceremony. Now that my father is recovered enough, they want to make things official.

Mom's face goes slack. "How could he find out?"

"Our walls are thin as paper," says Dad.

"He's right," I offer. "I can hear the worshippers outside. No doubt, they eavesdrop on us, too."

"It's not on purpose!" calls a voice through the kitchen window. It sounds a lot like tracksuit grandma. "And you never gave me an answer about that armpit autograph."

I shake my head. It's definitely tracksuit grandma. My life is so weird.

On the little television, the Greek gasps. "Are you certain about this wedding?"

Foster pulls out sheet of paper. Even from a distance, I can tell that the thing clearly has spaghetti stains on it. *The official approval for marriage from Heavenly Chapel.* I remember seeing it on the kitchen counter. Someone must have thrown it out. Which is even nastier.

I wince. "Or, Foster could also be picking through our trash. Eew."

The Greek scans the sheet. "This document is official. The wedding will really take place."

Foster leans forward, bracing his elbows on his knees. This is the pose he uses during emergency meetings about Havoc attacks. "We ghouls value our traditions," declares Foster. "Someone as important as the Great Scala should not be a bastardess."

Shock ripples across my skin. "Wait. Did he just call me a bastardess?" Every kid I know just saw that.

"And then we have sacred rituals like marriage," continues Foster. "They aren't ghoul. They aren't quasi. No, such rites make up the very fabric of what it means to be from Purgatory. We can't allow something this important to pass by without celebrating. That's why I'm sponsoring a parade in the Scala's honor this Friday —I call it the Non-Bastardess Festival."

Rage burns through my nervous system. My eyes flare red. And did he just name a freaking parade the *Non-Bastardess Festival?* I point at the television set. "You're dead to me, Commander Starling."

Dad pales. "Don't kill anyone, please."

"Not to worry, Xav," explains Mom. "She's adjusting."

Back on screen, the camera zooms in on the Greek. "As Heraclitus said, there is nothing permanent except change. See you tomorrow!"

Dad clicks off the television. "I'm sorry." His gaze flickers between me and Mom. "For both of you."

Mom makes a 'shh' face and leads us all over to the kitchen table. I get what she means. We can't keep talking in loud voices. Who knows what my worshippers will hear? Instead, we all huddle for a quick whisper-fest.

"That celebrity has no idea how to run a realm," says Mom in a low voice. "He's only following orders from the Oligarchy."

Dad nods. "It's a solid plan, even if it is from the Oligarchy. This parade makes the referendum about our marriage, not what's best for Purgatory. Trouble is, there are serious issues facing this realm. The government needs revamping. Demons still stalk the streets. We don't even have a military yet."

"And Foster is announcing this so close to voting day," I state. "That's not coincidence."

"No, they're waiting until the last minute on purpose," says Mom. "We don't have enough time to counteract this Foster fellow."

I try to focus on all these revelations, but I can only think about one thing.

The Non-Bastardess Festival.

While my parents keep whisper-scheming, I grab the last box of Frankenberry cereal, pour the final crumbs into a bowl and chow down. Soon the sugar hits my system and with it, an idea. "Foster wants to celebrate?" I whisper-yell. "Let's give him what he wants."

Mom rubs her temples with her fingertips. "Not following."

"Let's do a big-ass wedding on Friday instead." I wave my spoon for emphasis. "Make his parade look like crap on a cracker."

"Big ass wedding?" repeats my father.

"Sure." More of my plan comes into focus. "You fly around in golden armor. Mom gives one of her awesome speeches. I'll make my igni do some cool stuff. We can even get the thrax to show up and ride around on horses. They look fabulous doing that."

"But by Friday?" Mom drums her nails on the table-top, which means she's considering this concept. "It's Wednesday. That's not a lot of time."

"Cissy can help you," says Dad.

Great point. My best friend wants to be the Diplo-matic Senator for Purgatory so badly, it isn't even funny. Aiding Mom with a rush wedding would be right up her alley.

I raise my hand. "Count me in for helping, too."

"You still need to recover, honey." Mom drums her fingers even faster. She's *really* thinking this through. "Get yourself a nice purple dress, that's all you need to do."

"So we're going through with this?" I ask.

My parents exchange a long look before Mom answers. "Yes, we are." She gives me the side eye. "And don't forget about the dress. I know how you hate gowns."

"Gowns-shmowns." I twiddle my fingers like I'm waving her concerns *buh-bye*. "Easy peasy."

Thud ... thud ... thud ...

Someone's at our front door. I set my cereal bowl aside. "I'll get it."

With that, I speed out of the kitchen. With every step, my head turns fuzzier with worry. What just happened back there? Did I really commit to buying a big purple dress and doing a huge public appearance on Friday?

Me and my big mouth.

3

$\mathcal{I}$ pull open the front door. Lincoln stands outside. He looks yummy in his jeans, heavy boots and tight grey Henley. *How I love casual day.* A smirk rounds his full lips. "And once again, it seems Harvey is on duty."

"Not buying the line that I'm in the middle of an emergency?"

"Nuh-uh."

"Hmm." I tap my chin dramatically. "What was that guard's name again?"

"Harvey. Round face. Mismatched eyes. Big ears. Is a total softie for my *girlfriend*."

My pulse spikes. This is the first time I've heard that particular word with such emphasis. It's very official-sounding and makes my insides turn to goo.

"Girlfriend?"

Behind him, the crowd on the front lawn gets rowdy. *Talk about ruining a moment.*

"Save my goldfish," cries one.

"Heal my tail," says a second.

"Fix my car battery!" calls a third.

Car battery? Seriously? I have some odd followers.

Gripping Lincoln's hand, I guide him inside. The moment the front door is closed, Lincoln presses me against the wall. "Girlfriend. Guiding star. Obsession." He leans in and nips my earlobe, which sends all kinds of flippy feelings through my insides. "I've given Harvey extra shifts, you know. If he keeps doing this, I may promote him to Captain."

I love the liquid-happy sensation that now runs through my soul. "You do that."

Mom calls in from the kitchen. "Who is it, honey?"

"Lincoln," I call.

"Oh, that's nice," Mom sounds totally distracted. "Did you tell him about the dress?"

Lincoln leans back. "Dress?"

You ever have a moment where you start talking and can't stop? It's like part of you floats outside your real body, trying to force your mouth to close. Well, that's exactly what happens to me right now.

"There's this douche-y ghoul named Foster who's

being a total dick," I explain. "He says I'm a bastardess and wants to throw a parade on Friday. Why? Because that's the day I'll no longer be illegitimate since my parents already planned their secret wedding. *Secret* being the key word in that sentence. Now it's totally out in the open. And this Anti-Bastardess Festival could derail Mom's chances to be President. So I had the idea to bump up the wedding, turn it into a bigger celebration, and steal Foster's thunder." I huff out of a breath. "All of which means I need to find a purple dressy-dress to wear by Friday."

Lincoln leans in, rubbing his nose along the length of mine. Not gonna lie. That feels mighty good.

"I can help with that," he says in a grumbly voice.

My brows lift. "You can?"

Lincoln gives me the barest of nods. Meanwhile, his grip on my waist turns even tighter. I get a feeling he has something sneaky planned.

I like where this is going.

Going up on tiptoe, I whisper in his ear. "Let's do it." *Oops, that came out sexier than I meant.*

"Don't leave before visiting the kitchen," calls Mom.

"We need to chat with Lincoln," adds Dad. "About horses for Friday."

Lincoln chuckles, the sound deep and low. "Horses

as well? Why, how helpful that I'm High Prince of the Thrax."

I weave my fingers through his. The touch of his skin is electric; so warm and rough, all at once. Together, we head toward the kitchen. Once there, Lincoln cracks a charm that looks like a postage stamp so we can all speak without whispering. What follows is a long conversation about horses. And carriages maybe. Perhaps some things about parade routes get thrown in there, too.

Not gonna lie. Planning events isn't my thing. My mind wanders, and when my thoughts take a vacation, they visit my favorite place: Demonville. Sure, I tried to get rid of all the evildoers, but there are still a ton of demons running around Purgatory. How can I get involved on cleaning things up around here? Maybe I can crank up some kind of thrax-style demon patrols? It's a thought.

At some point, I realize that everyone has stopped talking. *Yipes.* I blink hard and refocus. "What did I miss?"

"Nothing," says Mom. "We got it all figured out."

"Friday will be marvelous," says Dad. He emphasizes that point with one of his million-watt smiles, so I figure he really means it.

Lincoln gives my hand a squeeze. "Now, we go to Antrum."

My eyes widen. I've never visited Lincoln's home. "With all the thrax and everything?"

"That's the one," answers Lincoln.

I pause, considering. This is another big relationship-y thing. First being called girlfriend in a very deliberate way … and now visiting the homeland. Sure, it's underground and full of demon killers, but the point is the same.

Total relationship-y thing.

I smile my face off and give his hand a squeeze. "In that case, let's go."

4

It only takes a few minutes to change into my Scala robes and make my goodbyes. In short order, Lincoln and I are off for Antrum. The moment we open the front door, the crowds burst out cheering. They mean well, but they're very loud.

And pushy.

Not to mention grabby.

Long story short, there's some awkwardness to get past the mob. This time, Lincoln's guards are right on it, creating a channel for us to walk through. We quickly reach the sidewalk. I pause, noting the big-ass horse standing in the middle of my street.

"Nightshade is here," I say, stating the obvious. I can't help it, though. There are so many people around. And yet, my horse waits solo in the center of the pavement. No one nearby for yards.

Lincoln nods. "She's casting spells for invisibility and fear. Won't work forever, but it's a good start."

I purse my lips, impressed. I keep forgetting how Night can cast minor spells.

Best. Horse. Ever.

The crowd presses in closer. Harvey and the other guards are having a tough time keeping them back. No time to waste.

I make a wincey-face and for one reason: I'm not sure how this whole 'ride away plan' will work. "How long can Night keep us hid—"

Someone grabs a lock of my hair and yanks. Hard. Which brings up two things.

One, evidently Night can't keep us hidden for very long.

And two, my followers suck sometimes.

Gripping my hair, I yank it out of the random worshipper's grasp. A voice calls out from the crowd. "I got a hair! I shall be immortal!" More quasis tackle the speaker.

"On second thought, let's just get out of here," I say.

"Completely agree. Harvey and the others have their work cut out for them."

"I wish my Scala robes were battle suit. That would make this whole thing easier." All of a sudden, the threads tickle. The fabric of my Scala robes actually realigns. A moment later, I'm wearing white battle armor, complete with boots. Who knew my robes did that? Major job perk.

Lincoln sets his hand at the base of my spine. Together, he and I hustle our way through the crowd, making a beeline for Nightshade.

Out of nowhere, tracksuit grandma grabs my wrist. "If you won't sign my armpit, fine. I'm voting for Foster in Monday's election."

"Foster can't keep us safe from demons," cries a mother with a chunky baby on her hip. Both mom and baby have rattlesnake tails. I decide that I like them.

Tracksuit grandma's wrinkled face turns positively mean. "We'll see."

I give the mom a wide smile. "You're awesome, sister." I then look to tracksuit grandma. "You, not so much."

Lincoln pulls the old lady's grip off my arm. Before I know it, he's swung me onto Nightshade's saddle. Lincoln sits behind me, his chest pressing against my back. Not gonna lie. I'm really happy to have his solid body against mine. Much as I hate to admit it, my followers are really getting to me.

A pouf of purple smoke surrounds us. Night casts another spell.

A moment later, the nearby quasis wander about as if in a dream. Another chorus of comments fills the air.

"Where did she go?"

"The Great Scala has disappeared into Heaven."

Lincoln leans in to whisper in my ear. "Another vanishing spell."

I nod and smile. *Me likey.*

Someone calls out, "Let's do a chorus of *Glory, Glory Myla-lujah.* Maybe she'll return."

A sick taste fills my mouth. *Where do they come up with these ideas?* I whisper to Lincoln over my shoulder. "I really hate it when they start to sing." My tail agrees. It does that up-periscope move where it arches my shoulder, the arrowhead end scanning the crowd. Considering how it's my tail and all, I know what this particular move means.

Break into song and someone gets skewered.

Thankfully, no one tries to start the tune. Instead, Lincoln clicks his tongue and Night takes off at a slow pace. The crowd naturally parts for us as we step along. No question about it; being invisible is pretty awesome.

Soon we leave the streets of Purgatory behind and enter the woods that separate my house from Lincoln's old camp. The battle planning side of my brain kicks into high gear.

"So, we're hitting your old camp?"

He leans in and whispers in my ear, all growly-like. "We are."

I lean against his chest. It's super-comfortable. "Are the dresses there?"

"No, but there *is* an old Pulpitum station. We can use it to transfer to Antrum."

That perks me up. I haven't been in a Pulpitum before. "How does that work?"

Night keeps a leisurely pace across the countryside while Lincoln explains how Pulpitum are round metal platforms that hurtle through the ground. Its how thrax connect different realms while staying super-secure about who goes where because DEMONS. I get it.

In short order, Night approaches the old thrax camp. Being back here is like stepping through memories. As in: there's the spot where I fought the Arachnoid demon. And here's where I put on that poufy white dress. Oh, and that's the mead hall where Lincoln and I released the garbage demons. Good times.

A few thrax workers still mill about, filling wheelbarrows with stuff that got left behind. Lincoln greets everyone while remembering their names. He's amazing that way.

A thought hits me. Is perfect name-recall a requirement for leading your people? If so, then I'll definitely suck at my new job.

Lincoln's voice sounds all low and growly in my ear again. "Myla, we're here."

I shake my head, snapping back into the present moment. Night has stopped before a round tent set into the muddy earth. Lines of withering trees surround the structure. I slide off Night; Lincoln follows. Hand in hand, we step inside the tent.

For the record, it's beyond awesome walk around with my guy. It wasn't that long ago, my life was all about kicking ass in the Arena. My boy experiences were nil. Sure, there were those weird advances from Zeke, but those didn't count. Yet now, just marching around with Lincoln? It's suddenly natural and extraordinary, all at once.

The moment we step inside the tent, a small grid of light flashes across us. I've seen this kind of thing on TV shows. This is a high-tech way of checking ID. A round metal platform covers the floor. Lincoln guides us to stand at the disc's center while a young guy's voice echoes through the air.

"Greetings, Prince Lincoln."

My guy doesn't miss a beat. "Hello, Phineas."

Again, with the names. I make a mental note to ask

Lincoln how he remembers everyone. Maybe there's a trick I can pick up.

Sirens break the air, breaking up my thoughts. "Oh, no!" cries Phineas. "Demon alert!"

"This is Prince Lincoln Vidar Osric Aquilus. Deactivate Alert. This is no demon with me. It's the Great Scala."

"Are you certain?" asks Phineas.

"What does the queen tell you?"

"What?" Phineas gasps. "I mean, why would the queen be saying anything right now?"

Lincoln shakes his head. "Phineas. I know how Mother works. She was aware the moment I set foot inside the Pulpitum. Chances are, she's already reviewed the scans on Myla. Ask her if the Great Scala is approved to enter Antrum. I'll wait." Lincoln focuses on me. "Apologies for this. If I'd known you were returning with me, I'd have set things up to work far more smoothly."

"No worries. I'm just glad about the dress thing." *Truth.*

A new voice sounds through the tent. "What dress thing?" The voice is clipped, mature and female.

Octavia. And she's eavesdropping because, *of course she is.*

"Hello, Mother. No doubt, you've heard about the expanded wedding event for Myla's parents."

"Yes," says Octavia.

I frown. That conversation just took place. How could Octavia possibly know? Then again, I consider Lincoln's mother. She knows.

"Myla and I must find her a gown for Friday," explains Lincoln. It's a little odd to have a conversation with a disembodied voice in a tent, but that's what's happening.

"You'll go to Lady Midnight," says Octavia.

"Obviously," agrees Lincoln.

My brows lift. If you're going to be forced into a fancy dress, it feels better to have it come from someone named Lady Midnight.

Voices sound. Evidently, there's a lot of chatter going on at Phineas' side of things.

"Excuse me," adds Octavia. "I'm at transfer central now. Operations here are less than smooth here. There's unclear rotation schedules, messy workstations and foodstuffs laying around." Octavia huffs. "And did someone put wet socks on the console?"

"That was me," squeaks Phineas. "I stepped in a puddle on the way over."

When Octavia next speaks, her words drip with menace. "Take the socks off the console. Then we'll talk.

This is why I do spot checks of your facilities here at Transfer Central. Let's have a little discussion about efficiency and cleanliness."

I look to Lincoln. He mouths two words: *ass kicking.*

Through the hidden speakers, I hear the sounds of people scrambling around.

Oh, yeah. Asses will be kicked indeed.

"Yes, your Majesty," says someone in transfer central.

"Right away, Queen Octavia." That's Phineas again, and he sounds downright terrified.

For her part, Octavia clears her throat. "You'll find Lady Midnight at the Temple Of The First Gateway."

I cup my hand by my mouth. "That's, uh, great. Thanks."

A pause follows. When Octavia speaks again, there's an edge to her voice that could cut ice. "And you're not transferring my son and the Great Scala to the temple … why?"

The next voice we hear is a very frightened Phineas. "Starting transfer in Three … Two … One."

Lincoln entwines my fingers in his. Beneath our feet, the platform lurches to life. I clasp Lincoln's hands even more tightly as we hurtle off into the earth.

I'm about to see Antrum at last.

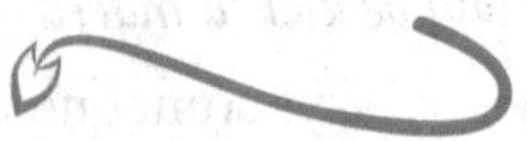

The Pulpitum platform careens through the ground. While keeping a firm grip on Lincoln's hands, I watch the play of earth, minerals and lava speed past. *So beautiful.*

Seconds later, the metal disc slams to a halt.

A minute ago, Lincoln and I waited inside a tent. Now we stand within a large room made from smooth sandstone. All around, the walls are covered in brightly-colored murals of men and women from ancient Egypt. Everyone's painted in profile-style as they drag long boats around. With that, I know one thing for certain.

We're here.

The Temple Of The First Gateway.

After that, it gets even better. There's only one other

person in the chamber with us: a woman with dark skin, high cheekbones and aristocratic features. She wears a white sheath decorated in glittering beads. A matching turban sits atop her head.

"Lady Midnight," says Lincoln.

"Your Highness." Lady Midnight has a soft and feminine voice. She's one of those people who seems to whisper, yet her voice carries over everyone else's anyway. "Welcome to the House of Horus."

I'm still learning about the different thrax houses, but I remember that Horus comes from ancient Egypt and uses chariots in battle. That explains the painted murals and large stone chamber. All in all, this room is like an Egyptian tomb, minus the dead bodies and whatnot.

Lady Midnight flicks her gaze to me. She's got wide brown eyes that stare right through you. On instinct, I bow my head. It feels like the right move.

"Lady Midnight," I say.

"Call me Dee," she instructs.

"Sure thing. Thanks for helping me out."

"I'm the Mistress of Beauty for Queen Octavia … among other things. It's my pleasure to assist." Turning, she strolls across the stone floor. "This way."

A million questions whir through my head. What's a

Mistress of Beauty? Why do they call this place the Temple Of The First Gateway? And how does all this help me get dressed for Friday? But I set my questions aside for now. Dee is one those people where when she says *this way*, you don't launch into a ton of chatter.

A small rectangular arch is set into the base of the far wall. Dee steps through it. Lincoln and I follow. The opening leads to a snug stone hallway that ends in a rock wall. Dee sets her hand against the stone. "Dressing chambers," she says.

The wall glistens with bronze light. I've seen this effect before, only usually it's purple. But whatever the color, there's no question what's happening now. *Magic.* A moment later, the wall disintegrates into a cascade of bronze dust. Surprise prickles across my skin.

That's a mighty impressive trick.

Dee steps through the newly-vanished wall and into a chamber made from mahogany wood. A screen divides the room. On the left side, there stands a wall of mirrors. On the right, there's a wooden bureau.

"Open the wardrobe and you'll find various gowns I've chosen for you," explains Dee.

I pull at the neckline of my Scala roles. "Can I wear these underneath?"

In reply, Dee gives me a look that can only be described as, *Hell no.* It's as if I asked if I could dribble catsup on the gowns. Moving quickly, I lift my palms in the universal gesture for, *forget I asked.* "You know what? I don't need Scala robes. That's fine."

"But they help you focus your powers," says Lincoln.

I shrug. "On Friday, I'll be doing the equivalent of a laser light show, not moving souls around. No worries."

Lincoln narrows his eyes in my direction. I already told him my powers have been off lately. My guy is definitely in what I consider his Captain Protective mode. We haven't been dating for long, but I do know one thing. Lincoln won't let this drop.

"Excellent," says Dee. "Do you require any servants?"

I tilt my head. "Like to bring me snacks?"

"Not food." A small smile rounds Dee's mouth. "They can help you get dressed."

"Oh." I wince. "No, thanks. I've been dressing myself for a while now."

Dee's grin widens. "In that case, I wonder if it would be acceptable for me to depart. A certain earl has made some troublesome requests for the upcoming Ceremony Of The Trickster's Gate."

Funny how she doesn't have to say, Earl of Acca, and I know exactly who she's talking about.

"Feel free to leave," says Lincoln. "I'll join you as soon as I can."

Dee steps out through the same not-a-wall where we

just entered. The moment she moves into the shadows, the area glistens with bronze light once more. One second, it's an open space. The next, the spot has transformed into a single panel of mahogany with a single door. Magic is the bomb.

I turn to Lincoln. "I have so many questions, I don't even know where to begin."

Lincoln grabs my hands and swings them between us. "Start anywhere you like."

So we play a quick game of questions and answers. Turns out, Lady Midnight makes people and events lovely—that's what it means to be the Mistress of Beauty. Specifically, Dee decorates all of Octavia's balls and supplies her gowns. Plus, Dee wields special magic from ancient Egypt. Only a handful of folks from Horus have this power, and it always shows as bronze. Which brings me to my next set of questions.

"What was with all the boats and gates?" I hitch my thumb toward the main chamber where we landed. "The walls were covered with ancient Egyptians dragging them around."

Lincoln lifts his hand. "Let's say this is a boat. In ancient Egypt, they call it a barque. Every night, the god Ra sails this boat through twelve different gateways to ensure the sun rises again in the morning." Lincoln moves his boat-hand into a circle. "Each gate has a monster that must be fought in order to ensure the sun rises in the morning."

I raise my hand. "For the record, I heard blah-blah-blah-monster-blah-blah-blah."

"I'd expect nothing else."

"If this barque thing really exists, I'm down with joining."

Lincoln chuckles. "There hasn't been a real solar barque for ages. But there are temples and ceremonies for each gateway. The largest ritual is for the Trickster's Gateway, which Dee is working on."

"And that's where you're supposed to be right now."

"I'm taking a break. It's not a problem."

"But Acca is always trouble."

Lincoln leans against a nearby stretch of wall on the other side of the divider. "I'm waiting to see your first dress." He folds his arms over his chest. It's his way of saying that he's not going anywhere.

For the record, I love this idea.

My eyes widen. "Getting dressed. Right." All of a sudden, I realize I'm about to become mostly naked in an empty room with Lincoln. Parts of me start tingling. "So I just open that bureau thingy then?" I point to the wardrobe in question, which is on the other side of the privacy screen.

Lincoln's gaze turns intense. "Yes. Just keep opening until you see what you like."

"Okay." I try to sound casual, but the word comes out as more of a peep than anything else.

Damn you, hormones.

The bureau itself is a tall wooden thing with a set of doors on the front. I pull them open and—WHOA—there's more magic. A cascade of bronze lights fills the open wardrobe.

I suck in a shaky breath. "That's amazing."

"The dress?"

"No, the glitter show. People must come from all around to see this bronze sparkle stuff."

"Actually, the opposite is true. The fireworks mean nothing. What's important is what lies hidden inside."

The words echo through my mind in strange ways.

The fireworks mean nothing. What's important is what lies hidden inside.

This sound effect isn't coming from me. No, it's my igni who are making the phrases go on auto-repeat inside my skull. I press my hands on my temples. "I got it guys, you like what Lincoln said."

My igni take this moment to screech inside my brain.

Sadly, this is the dark igni, the ones who transfer souls to Hell. Right now, their voices remind me of that time the brakes snapped on Betsy, my POS station wagon.

"What's wrong?" asks Lincoln.

"My igni."

"Do you need help?"

"No, I'm good." In an act of kindness from the universe, my igni shut the fuck up. Shaking my head, I focus on the interior of the bureau. A simple purple sheath hangs inside. I may not be Gown Girl, but I know what looks good on me. This style is for someone who's skinny as a bone. The Great Scala's got curves.

Time to try again.

I close the door and open it a second time. More bronze glitter shows before revealing a massive pouf dress made with miles of purple skirt. It's like a ballerina's tutu on steroids.

No, thank you.

Crossing my fingers, I close the door once more. When I open it again, there's the now-standard shower of glimmering magic. But there's also a kick-ass gown inside. The design is simple with no shoulders, a straight neckline, and a floor-length skirt that's not poufy so much as feminine. There's even a pair of matching purple gloves. Before I know it, I've whipped off my

Scala robes and slipped into the gown. There's only one step left.

The back zipper.

Normally, I don't wear stuff that zips up the back. Or has zippers at all, actually. The ghouls always had us in sweats. But the few times that back-zippers have entered my life, my tail has always done the honors. Which is why I tap my tail right now. It isn't easy to do while holding up the front of your gown, but I manage.

"Can you help me?" I ask.

In reply, my tail does its ahoy-periscope move. The arrowhead end waves from side to side. *No.*

"Come on," I whisper.

My tail points toward Lincoln's side of the room. The meaning is clear. *Get help from the Prince or nothing.*

I shift my weight from foot to foot. Nervous energy zings through my insides. I was so pumped to find a cute dress, I forgot all about *the hot boyfriend across the room* side of the equation. My legs turn gooey beneath me. Dumb limbs.

With shaky steps, I walk past the partition screen. My hands grip the front of my dress so tightly, I worry that I might tear the fabric. The moment I step into Lincoln's line of sight, I can see the severity of my error here.

He looks all casual and cute as he leans against the

wall in his perfectly worn-in jeans that curve *just so* around his well-toned legs. Plus, that Henley makes his shoulders seem especially wide. And best of all, my guy stares at me with raw intensity.

How did I get so lucky?

At this point, my lust demon stirs inside me. Desire heats my veins. All I can think about is one question: what would it be like to kiss Lincoln again? Will he brush his lips gently across mine … or pull me into a fierce kiss?

Some small part of me screams that I came to this side of the room for a reason. I just can't think what that purpose is anymore.

Not sure I care, either.

Lincoln kicks off the wall and strides in my direction. "Need some help with the zipper?"

For a moment, I'm at a loss. I wanted kisses, not a zipper. Then, I remember. That's right. I'm here for the dress. I clear my throat and try not to look like someone who's thinking with her hormones. "Yes, thanks."

There, that sounded mature and logical.

Lincoln moves to stand behind me. He brushes his fingertips along the seam between the opened gown and my bare back. Dang, that sets off serious fireworks for my inner lust demon.

"This fabric is so soft," my guy says, all rumbly-like.

My tail takes the chance to do a reverse up-periscope, which is where the arrowhead shaped end points at my face. Now it's doing an up and down movement that means, *yes, yes, yes.*

I'm woman enough to take direction from my tail. "Yes, it is," I agree.

Lincoln grips the base of the zipper and slowly pulls it up. His fingers brush along my skin with the movement. I swear, I never imagined that it could be sexy to put clothes *on*, but my guy works this scene like a pro. Once done, he steps around me, keeping a butterfly-soft touch on my skin as he goes.

Back.

Shoulder.

Throat.

"This looks beautiful on you," he says in a husky voice.

"Thanks." Honestly, I'm amazed I got a word out.

Lincoln then runs his fingers up my neck, pausing when his touch frames my face. My heart pounds away at double speed as my guy pulls me in for a deep kiss. Not a brush of the lips. Yet nothing too rough, either. Lincoln's tongue caresses mine in a slow dance of plea-sure. My inner lust demon roars with delight.

Then he stops. *Boo.*

I've been through this situation once before, back when Lincoln and I were sharing the kiss of our lives in a darkened mead hall. As a result, I have a pretty good idea what to expect here. A weight of disappointment settles on my shoulders. "Let me guess. Octavia is coming."

Lincoln nods and steps back.

Behind us, the wooden door swings open. Sure enough, Octavia speeds into the room. As always, she looks prim and lethal with her neat gray chignon and black velvet gown.

"My son," Octavia air-kisses Lincoln's cheek before turning to me. "So nice to see you, my dear." She leans back and eyes me closely. "You look positively lovely, child."

I grin. Octavia is a lot of things, but she isn't a liar, especially when it comes to something as important as formal gowns. Knowing she likes this dress? Total score.

"Thank you," I say.

Octavia sighs. "How I wish the color of Rixa were purple, like Purgatory. Black gets so monotonous."

"How goes the planning with Camilla and Xavier?" asks Lincoln.

I notice that my guy doesn't even question if his mother is knee-deep in scheming with my parents.

Instead, he launches right into the update. Does my guy know his mom or what?

"It's all set," says Octavia with a wave of her hand. "We'll do a real parade before the ghoul thing starts. There will be horses. Warriors. You. It'll be stunning." She looks to me. "Your friend Cissy has been extraordinarily helpful."

I smile. "Glad to hear it." Behind me, my tail curls its arrowhead-shaped end. That's its way of crossing fingers for Cissy to become the Senator for Diplomacy. We both want that for her, big time.

Octavia rounds on Lincoln. "You were supposed to be at the council for planning the Trickster's Gate Ceremony today. Acca is acting strangely."

"I heard," Lincoln has his unreadable face on. I'm guessing he hates the concept of babysitting Aldred, which makes my guy's calm demeanor even more impressive. "I'll get Myla safely home and then deal with the Earl."

"That will suffice, so long as you're speedy about it." Octavia straightens the folds of her black gown. "In that case, I'll see you both safely back to the platform." The queen eyes me carefully. The words are there if unspoken. *No more smooching my son when he needs to take down the Earl of Acca.* Not that I blame her.

That Aldred is a dick.

So I scoot to the other side of the screen, change back into my Scala robes and get ready to return to Purgatory. All the while, I can't help but smile. In the great game of life, I'm now up one purple gown and a serious session of kissing.

That's what I call a good day.

6

Soon Octavia, Lincoln and I stand inside the Temple Of The First Gateway again. The metal of the Pulpitum platform gleams before us in the dim light. Now that I'm ready for my return trip to Purgatory, my thoughts circle back to Foster.

What is his deal anyway?

An image pops into my mind from this morning. It's Foster on the little TV in my kitchen, and he's smiling his face off. Sure, the guy's an actor, but nobody is that good. He's totally into becoming President.

And stopping my family.

And holding an anti-bastardess parade in my honor.

What a douchebag.

Lincoln and I move to stand in the center of the

round transfer platform. Octavia waits just beyond the disc's edge.

"Hurry back, Lincoln," she warns. "You know how Aldred can be."

Lincoln nods. "That I do."

Octavia snaps her fingers. "Phineas, I know you're listening. Begin the countdown, please."

Turning to me, Lincoln takes my hands in his. He gives me the barest of winks as Phineas' voice sounds once more. "Starting transfer in three … two … one."

Beneath our feet, the metal disc lurches to life. The platform speeds off past all sorts of stuff. There's some magma. Maybe a line of diamonds of two. And tons of dirt. Mostly, I avoid the view outside the disc. Instead, I look into Lincoln's mismatched eyes and wish Octavia didn't have such crap luck interrupting us.

Thud! The platform comes a halt inside the round tent of the deserted thrax camp. The air holds a damp chill; that means it's probably early evening. How do I know these things? They say human Eskimos have hundreds of words for snow. When you live in Purgatory, it's like that, only with rain and humidity.

Hand in hand, Lincoln and I walk through the tent-flap door. Once outside, a light drizzle flecks my skin with mist. Overhead, the clouds are an especially dark shade of gray. The edge of cold bites into my skin.

Yup, it's early evening. I totally called it.

On reflex, I scan the line of dying trees and search for any sign of Nightshade. A whinny sounds nearby. My horse is close, but not here and ready to ride. I haven't known Night for long, but I do know one thing. If she's not ready to go, then there's a reason.

What does Night know that I don't?

That's when I see it.

Odd patterns in the dying grass.

Smouldering paw prints.

A demon trail.

Lincoln kneels down, brushing his fingertips against the earth. No doubt about it. My guy is now in *demon hunting mode.* I couldn't be happier. Choosing dresses and dealing with demanding queens? Not my thing.

Killing stuff is so much better.

Lincoln brushes the soil between his thumb and pointer finger. "Infernus demon tracks," he says in a low voice.

I pump my fist in the air. "Yes!"

Lincoln rises. "Shall we?"

Oh, how I love this idea. *Lincoln and I, off on a demon hunt.* That said, I'm also trying to be more goddess-like now. Therefore, I slap on my most mature and serious face. "Shouldn't you go back to Antrum for some, uh, Aldred gunk?"

Okay, the mature stuff went a little sideways at the end there. All in all, it was still a good effort, though. I mean, two months ago, who would have thought I'd pause before chasing down a demon?

Lincoln scans the ground more closely. "I should. Leaving Aldred alone is only asking for trouble. And the Trickster's Gateway Ceremony is very important."

That's what Lincoln says.

What my guy does, however, is *not* get up from a kneeling position. If anything, Lincoln is even more focused on the demon trail before us.

"But you aren't returning to Antrum, are you?"

Rising, Lincoln pulls his baculum from the waistband of his jeans. "Not a chance."

Fact: I have been super-mature to point out that Lincoln should return to Antrum. But isn't the Earl of Acca *constantly* plotting something evil? Lincoln can't follow that creepster around 24-7.

Especially when there are demons to find.

"Care to choose the pathway?" asks Lincoln.

"Not my thing," I explain. "Tracking stuff in the wild isn't my strong suit. The demons I fight just sashay out onto the Arena floor." I ask my Scala robes to turn into badass battle armor, and they do it once more. Nice.

Lincoln eyes me from head to toe. "Meant to comment on that before. Seeing your robes change is something." That hungry look returns to my guy's eyes. For a moment, I debate about kissing Lincoln in the woods, but did I mention there's an Infernus demon nearby? Because there is. And I've never even seen one of those before.

Long story short, the smooching can wait. Sometimes the *wrath* part of my lust-and-wrath combo simply wins out, end of story.

I give my hips a little shimmy, though, just because I can. "I'm awesome and I know it. Now let's go kill stuff."

Lincoln winks. "In that case, follow me."

My guy and I take off into the woods. There's a lot of zipping around tree trunks, stomping into puddles and avoiding piles of slimy leaves. Eventually, we reach the mouth of a cave. The scent of charcoal turns overwhelming.

Even I know this is the demon's home. I bounce on the balls of my feet. *Yes!* Sure, I've fought evil in the Arena, but it's totally different to get some genuine lair action. No wonder the thrax love demon patrol.

Lincoln kneels before the cave entrance. He does that thing again where he pats the ground before rubbing earth between his fingers.

"There are no demons here."

"Seriously?" I rush inside the cave. Sure enough,

there's zero sign of any *big bads*. My shoulders slump. Total bummer.

After stepping inside as well, Lincoln gestures to the cave walls. "See those burn marks?"

"They're in a pinwheel pattern."

"That's the sign of an Infernus. No other fire demon leaves marks like those."

"How long has it been gone?"

"Hard to tell. There are too many tracks." He frowns. "Other hunters arrived here first."

"Thrax?"

"No, it looks like quasis. There are some drag marks from tails."

My brows lift with surprise. "That's weird. What my people know about demons is nil."

Lincoln scans the wall marks more closely. "You once told me demons volunteered to fight in the Arena. Perhaps the quasis who came here were part of that recruiting effort." Lincoln holds up a dark thread between his fingers. "I see signs that ghouls were here as well. There are remnants from their robes."

I bob my head, thinking this though. "That's possible. Sheila the Limus demon is a buddy of mine who worked the Arena. I never thought to ask how she got recruited." I tap my cheek and think things through. "One thing doesn't add up, though."

Lincoln turns to look in my direction. Damn, he's so cute with the charcoal smudge that now lines his cheek. "What's that?"

"Arena demons—meaning the ones on payroll—are only there to fool evil souls. They may look bad, but can't fight a lick. That's how it was with Sheila. But Infernus demons are nasty with a capital N. It doesn't fit the pattern."

"Now that the ghouls are leaving, perhaps things are changing in the Arena."

"Could be." I'm about to add that the ghouls have no intention of leaving when a new voice sounds.

"Hello in there!"

A jolt of recognition moves through me. I know that tone. Moving with dream-like steps, I find myself shuffling outside again.

And there he is.

Foster Reins.

And he's even wearing his silver Commander onesie.

For a moment, elation zings through my nervous system. After all, this is the guy who defeated the Havoc serpent of Sector Fifty-Nine. He outsmarted the great roach monster of the Scorpion Quadrant. He even helped the people of Planet Double X find a new star system to call home, which they totally needed after the cruelty of the Havoc Wars.

But all those happy vibes only lasts a few seconds, though.

Because there really is no Commander Starling.

The guy before me is an freaking loser who's holding a bastardess parade in my honor. Rage heats my blood.

You are so going down, buddy.

I fold my arms over my chest. "What do you want?"

Foster gives me a dazzling smile. "We haven't met. I'm Foster Reins, demon hunter."

I roll my eyes. "Kiss my ass, you lying liar."

That shuts him up.

Lincoln moves to stand beside me. My guy has his *stony-n-serious* face on. I've been on the receiving end of that look. It's not fun.

Foster rounds on Lincoln. "And you're the High Prince of the demon fighting thrax. What a treat to meet you as well. Now we can chat together as demon hunters."

Lincoln narrows his eyes. "You caught the Infernus?"

"Absolutely," answers Foster. The way his eyes glimmer with such confidence, it's clear that he's lying his ass off. "I just wanted to chat while we were all together. I already captured the Infernus demon, obviously. But if *you* were going to catch one, what would *you* do?"

A realization hits me. "I know what this us about." I

snap my fingers, trying to recall the statistic. "I've remember this from the TV. 93% of population thinks my family's better at fighting demons than anyone else. So you're trying to—*what?*—capture an Infernus before Friday and prove everyone wrong?"

Foster lifts his chin. "I don't know what you're talking about. I was just out for a walk, that's all."

Sure, he was just out for a walk.

Foster steps closer. "Running across you here, it's quite the happy accident. I've been wanting to talk to you alone anyway."

On reflex, I take a half-step backward. Something about Foster just sets off my eew-o-meter.

"Talking to the Great Scala alone?" Lincoln steps between Foster and me. "That's not happening."

I shoot Lincoln a thumbs-up before making a lewd hand gesture at Foster. "I am so not talking to you. You named a freaking parade after the fact that I'm a bastardess."

"Don't you want to hear what I have to say?" asks Foster innocently. "You must be a fan. Everyone is."

"No one remembers you." *Major lie.*

"Maybe they're forgotten me, but not for long."

That launches another realization. "Ah, haaaaa!" Stepping out from behind Lincoln, I point right at

Foster's nose. "You're totally doing this for the attention. That's really shallow."

Muscles feather along Foster's chiseled-yet-overly-pale jawline. "I was going to be friendly, but that won't work. We must talk. It could prove crucial for your parents."

And damn. Now I totally have to listen to Foster. My father just spent two decades getting tortured by Armageddon. Mom spent the same amount of time in her own version of Hell. Now both of them are working hard to fix Purgatory. If I can get some info to help them, I have to try.

I loop my hand in circles. "Spill."

"Your father's off sneaking around on your mother," declares Foster.

"Not believable," I deadpan. "Try again."

Foster raises in arm and gestures toward the horizon. It's his Commander Starling move that says what he's about to say is an order. "Your parents can't go through with this public wedding festival."

I shrug. "Not my call. Anything else?"

"Well, I don't want to embarrass you."

I roll my hand again. "Really."

"Weddings are complex," says Foster. "Anything can happen. This could all blow up in your parent's faces. And honestly? Your people are not ready for self-rule."

Heat pools behind my eyes. I have so had it with this *quasis can't take care of themselves* stuff. "What do you mean?"

"Quasis like you are simple folk." His voice takes on the tone of an adult addressing a toddler who piddled on the floor. "Someone must take care of you."

Lincoln takes my hand. Our gazes lock. He mouths three words, *you got this.*

And do I ever.

A lifetime of ghoul-related rage charges through my nervous system. "If most quasis can't run government it's because we were trained to serve you ghouls, not think for ourselves. Now is our chance to reclaim our home."

"But quasis are part demon." Foster says that like our demonic-ness is the obvious reason why we suck. That's yet another pet peeve of mine.

"Meanwhile," I counter. "Your people are *totally* dead."

A smug look shines in Foster's all-black eyes. "And yet, I now have a 92% approval rating in the polls."

"Your polls can kiss my butt."

"Best to support me anyway. If I don't win, the Oligarchy could get rather angry."

"Meaning?"

Foster's smug look takes on a darker edge. "How are your powers lately? Any problems?"

I suck in a shaky breath. My igni have been off, but it's nothing I can't handle. All of a sudden, my recent fight with Armageddon combines with all the drama of the day. It adds up to me feeling a little woozy on my feet.

Once again, Lincoln steps back between me and Foster. "This conversation is over," says the Prince.

At those words, Night prances into the clearing and whinnies. A small pouf of purple smoke rises. More magic. One moment, Lincoln and I are standing on the ground. The next, we're back in the saddle and prancing away from Foster. I don't even bother to look back. Who cares what that jerk ghoul is doing?

Lincoln and I ride on through the deepening night. Thoughts of Foster and my igni keep churning around my head. It's making me nuts. Eventually, Lincoln leans in to whisper in my ear. "Care to talk about it yet?"

"About what? I've nothing to talk about." *Maybe.*

He kisses the top of my ear. "I'm here when you're ready."

How does Lincoln know me so well? If the Prince had demanded that I spill my guts, then I'd have clammed right up. But since my guy is being so sweet, words just tumble from my mouth.

"It's like this," I say. "My igni are acting super strange these days. Sometimes they don't show up when I summon them, which hey, I get it. Maybe they're bathing their little igni sparkle bodies or whatever it is they do when they're alone."

"True," says Lincoln solemnly.

"And when my igni *do* want to show up, I always hear them first. They sound like music, voices or noise. So that's the system. But lately, their little voices are muted in my head. It's like they want to show up, but can't. And every time, their voices get a little harder to hear." A weight of sorrow settles into my heart. My igni are part of me. It hurts to think of them as trying to reach me, but unable to break through.

"And you suspect the ghouls."

"Well, the Oligarchy and I haven't exactly been hanging around, braiding each others hair and sharing secrets. Not that the Oligarchy have hair, but you get the idea."

"Clearly." I can't see my guy behind me. Even so, there's no mistaking the smile in his voice.

Twisting my torso, I give Lincoln the side eye. "Are you laughing at me?"

"Never. I only wish everyone had such colorful turn of phrase. It would make my life infinitely more interesting." A sneaky light shines in his mismatched eyes. "Then again, I could find a way to keep you around."

For the record, I love the direction this conversation is taking.

Night halts. I scan my surroundings. Dang. We're just a few streets away from my house now. No time for a major chat about our relationship even though, let's face it, I want to keep Lincoln around as well. Trouble is, my followers have some kind of Myla-radar. Any second now, they'll show up and ruin the moment.

My heart sinks. Hanging with Lincoln has been fun. Now I have to face reality, which is more than my kooky worshippers. It's the fact that, unless we win this election, the ghouls might keep my people in virtual slavery forever.

Lincoln leans in, pressing his chest against my back. "We have a day until Friday, Myla. We'll figure this out."

"This is all too much, too fast. I don't know what to do."

"Fortunately, I have a plan."

I perk right up. "You do?"

"Well, there's only one option when it comes to managing ghouls."

Twisting, I glance over my shoulder and meet Lincoln's gaze. *Of coooooourse. Why didn't I think of this before?* We share a slow smile as I say one word.

"Walker."

My honorary older brother is a ghoul genius. Whatever those undeadlies have planned, Walker is ten steps ahead of them, minimum.

Lincoln nods. "Precisely. And fortunately for you, I happen to know where Walker lives. I'll stop by on my way back to Antrum."

"You're the best." Shifting my weight, I move to give him a kiss. Lincoln shakes his head.

"What's wrong?" I ask.

"We have company."

I scan the surrounding street. Sure enough, a few dozen worshippers now surround us. Poor Harvey pushes through the crowd. The guy looks ready to cry. "Great Scala, would you like an escort home?"

"Thanks, Harvey. I would." I kiss Lincoln's cheek and slide off Night.

"See you soon," says Lincoln. After that, he and Night take off for Walker's place, wherever that is. I frown. One thing I've discovered about being a demi-goddess. Too many of my kisses seem to get interrupted.

Once Lincoln is gone, Harvey and the other guards walk me home. The good news is that this particular group of worshippers are a quiet bunch. No one tries to pull my hair or ask me to sign body parts, which is a total bonus. I should have enjoyed the silence because once I get inside my house, the place is a total freaking zoo. Cissy's here, along with about fifty other people. Everyone's planning the big extravaganza that is Friday. Whoa.

After a quick round of checking in, I speed into my bedroom, pull on a nightshirt and scooch under the covers. The moment my head hits the pillow, I can't believe how tired I feel. It's like every cell in my body is crying for sleep.

Turns out, what Mom said this morning is totally right. I'm still recovering from fighting Armageddon. I definitely need my rest.

7

*J*ust after dawn, a familiar and super-deep voice breaks up my rest.

"Myla, you are called to serve."

I sit bolt upright, my head spinning. "Who? What? How?"

Sure enough, Walker stands at the foot of my bed. He wears his ghoul robes and a smug smile. I point right at his nose. "You suck."

"That's vampires. I'm a ghoul."

"Hardy har har." I pause. "Is it me, or is it strangely quiet around here?"

"Everything *is* silent. I relocated the planning party to an abandoned library near the parade route."

I exhale. *No more fifty people running around the house.* "You're the best." I pull back the curtains. Sure enough, the thrax guards are there. I rub my eyes, not believing what else I'm seeing.

No one else is on my lawn. "Where are the worshippers?"

"Why? Do you miss them?"

I tilt my head. "What do you think?"

"I hired a body double who's at the library. Lucas, the earl of Striga, enchanted the tail and everything." At these words, my real tail pops up from under the covers to gesture wildly at Walker. I pat it soothingly. "Calm down, boy. Walker's not trying to steal your attention, just keep us sane."

Walker raises his arm. For the first time, I notice that he has an extra set of ghoul robes in his fist. "We have an appointment this morning." He tosses me the robes. "You and I shall the visit the secret warehouse where Foster Reins is planning his parade."

I grip the robes against my chest. "And I'll be disguised as a ghoul?"

Walker nods. "The robes are enchanted. In case you're counting, you now owe Lucas two favors."

"Lucas, Shmoocas." I pump my fist in the air. There's nothing like trying to act more mature to make fist-pumps all the more attractive. "Yes! One Myla the ghoul, coming up."

"And your Frankenberry cereal is on the kitchen counter. Once you've eaten, we can leave."

"Let me get this straight. You found Foster's hidden lair, got me a disguise, made all the annoying people go buh-bye, and even got me a fresh box of my favorite cereal?"

"Correct."

"Dang. You truly are amazing."

"I know. Now get dressed so we can get into trouble."

This may be greedy of me, but since Walker planned out everything else, I can't help but ask. "Is anyone *else* coming with us?"

Walker shakes his head. "Lincoln must deal with Aldred today."

"That's fine. Totally okay." I pause. "You know what? I take it back."

Walker tilts his head. "Are you going on a tirade?"

"Hells yeah."

"Excellent." Walker loves *tirade time.*

"Here's the deal. Lincoln has parents with the *title* King and Queen. Those two monarchs can totally deal with their own Earl, but do they? No. They make my boyfriend stay underground instead of sneaking around in ghoul robes—which we both know he'd love to do— just because they're too afraid of some nasty old douchebag who fights Limus demons with projectiles."

In my book, the Earl will never live that one down. "Boom."

Walker sighs.

"What?" I ask. "Too much?"

"No," says Walker. "You summed up the situation perfectly. In the future, I certainly hope that you can be an advocate for Lincoln. He's not the only one who can run Antrum, you know."

"On it," I say. *And I am.*

In my opinion, Lincoln's been flying solo for too long. He needs a wing-girl with guts, and that would be me. I'm about to share this insight when my stomach decides to growl something fierce. I set my hands on my belly. "Oops. I didn't eat dinner last night."

Walker steps toward the door. "In that case, I'll see you shortly."

Once the door closes, I get dressed *quick like a bunny* and then head to the kitchen. It quickly becomes clear that my house is a little too quiet. My every bite of Frankenberry turns amazingly loud. But it's better than worshippers, so I adjust.

Soon, Walker and I leave the *Maison de Lewis* and take off for Foster's secret lair. Turns out, the place is in a no-portal zone section of Purgatory, so we have to use my station wagon Betsy to get there. Once we get in my POS vehicle, it's clear that—*surprise, surprise*—Walker even got the oil changed. Now, that's an honorary older brother for you. Someone's getting a free cough syrup cocktail, that's for sure.

It's just before lunchtime when Walker and I arrive at the lair in question. I'd say that Foster's warehouse is in a shitty part of town. But this is Purgatory, after all. Everything around here sucks. And since Armageddon razed half the realm, many buildings are even in worse shape. So Foster's place is at about *medium-shit-show* level.

Walker and I take care to park far away. The area's deserted and we don't want to advertise our arrival. It's then a short walk over cracked asphalt and piles of burned-out debris until we reach a long flat building made from corrugated metal. Hard to miss, really. It's the only structure left standing in a sea of rubble. Walker and I step closer, stopping when we reach a massive loop of water recently carved out of the ground.

I pause. *Wait, what? Water?*

"Walker," I say in a tone only he can hear. The robes hide my height and stuff, but they can't mask my voice. "Is that a moat?"

"It is," says Walker.

"Were you expecting this?" I ask.

"Decidedly not." Walker folds his arms into the loopy sleeves of his ghoul robes. "We're here to answer an ad for day labor. There was nothing mentioned about a moat."

I kick my toe closer to the water's edge. "Looks newly dug." I think back to the demon hunt yesterday. Infernus demons are made of (you guessed it) fire. If you catch one, it would make sense to have a moat to keep it trapped. Only, it really seemed like Foster didn't catch anything yesterday. Unless you count an attitude, that is.

Across the moat, a ghoul steps out from the front door of the warehouse. "Who's there?"

"We're here about the ad," replies Walker.

The ghoul turns to speak with someone inside the warehouse. A bunch of mumbling follows. I catch the words, "more day laborers." The ghoul chats up his buddy some more before returning his attention to me and Walker. "We'll send out the rowboat."

Now, I should be happy that our *sneaking around* plan is moving forward, but honestly? I'm still stuck on the fact that there is a freaking *moat.*

Soon, a baby faced ghoul rows up to us in a rickety boat. "Greetings. I am GRDN-9000."

I decide that's a crap name, so I silently give him a new one. *Gordon.*

"Greetings to you," says Walker smoothly. "We are ZJ-68 and YNR-32."

"Oh," says Gordon.

A pause follows. Lines of worry tighten around my throat.

Did we just expose ourselves?

I mean, ghouls have that whole Group Think situation. Gordon can read Walker's mind. In fact, it should be instantly clear that those names are fake and I'm no ghoul. But if Gordon suspects something, he doesn't show it. I take this as a sign of two things. One, Lucas is a good warlock. And two, Walker is an even better liar.

"Okay," says Gordon at last. "Climb in."

So we do.

Before I know it, we're back on solid ground and stepping inside the warehouse. It's a wide and open space with lots of small tables covered in piles of red fabric. Ghoul workers stand in lines before the tables, fiddling with crimson sheets.

Walker nods over to the workers. "What are you making there?"

I open my mouth, ready to answer. Thankfully Gordon beats me to it. "Havoc costumes. For the parade."

"What are the Havoc?" asks Walker.

Now, I literally pull my hood down and bite my lips together because, DAY-UM, I want to answer that question. But my voice is decidedly un-ghoul-like. There's a particular undead rasp that you simply can't fake easily.

Okay, I could probably learn to mimic it if I tried but these are ghouls we're talking about here. Mimicking their voices just wasn't as effective at pissing them off. At least, not when compared to good old-fashioned sarcasm. A girl needs to have priorities.

Thankfully, Gordon jumps in to explain. "The Havoc are characters from a television show called Stellar One. You know, the series with Foster Reins?"

"Ah, Foster," says Walker sagely.

"Yes, Foster," echoes Gordon. The way he says those words, it's clear that Gordon isn't the pointiest Sharpie in the ghoul pen collection.

I fidget under my heavy ghoul robes. These things are way too itchy. Plus, it's getting really old to just stand around without talking. And did I mention that Gordon is still staring blankly at Walker? I really think I over-worried before, so I decide to let one little question slip out.

I point to a tall metal box that stands at the center of the warehouse floor. "And what's th—"

"YNR-32," interrupts Walker. "Don't injure yourself trying to speak. I know you lost your tongue in that horrible dental accident."

"Huh?" I ask.

"The horrible dental accident," says Walker slowly. "The one that happened just before you died and became a ghoul." He follows up that statement with what's supposed to be irritated look, but there's no real anger in it.

Still, the hint is taken. Once more, I point at the tall metal thingy. "Ugh, ugh," I say.

Gordon nods. "Yes YNR-32, I know what that thing is."

One second passes.

Two.

Three.

No one says anything.

"UGH!" This time, I grunt so loudly, a few heads turn in our direction.

"What my colleague means," says Walker smoothly, "is that we would very much appreciate it if you'd describe the purpose of that tall metal box."

"Oh!" Gordon smiles, and he's the kind of baby-faced guy who's missing at least two front teeth. "That's the trailer where we're putting in all the fireworks. And only the fireworks. Nothing else. Nope. Just fireworks. That's it."

Walker and I share a long look. Clearly, something is planned for that trailer which has nothing to do with fireworks.

Note taken.

Gordon pulls a clipboard from the folds of his ghoul robes. "I have some questions to ask before we begin."

"Not a problem," says Walker smoothly.

"First question. If given some diagrams, would you be able to assemble costumes for children?"

"Yes," says Walker.

"Ugh," I grunt.

"Assembly skills, check." Gordon scribbles on his clipboard. "Question two. This warehouse is a no-portal zone."

"This whole section of Purgatory is one, actually," corrects Walker.

"Right," says Gordon. "So you understand that you're here to work, not sneak off."

"What if I need to leave quickly?" asks Walker.

"We've a portal pad out back. But that's for emergencies only." Gordon tries to frown, but with his baby face, it just doesn't work. "Is that going to be a problem?"

"No," says Walker.

"Ugh," I add.

Gordon starts scribbling again. "Fine with no portals." He looks up. "Last question. Let's say you were going to work somewhere and that place is pretty deserted." Gordon stares at me and Walker expectantly. Evidently, we're supposed to say something. I nudge walker in the ribs.

"Deserted, got it," says Walker.

"Ugh."

"Now," continues Gordon. "If a demon were to murder you on the way to work, what would happen in that situation?"

Talk about your odd questions.

"Meaning?" asks Walker.

"Would anyone notice your death before a certain date?" asks Gordon. He glances around the warehouse, as if picking a day at random. "For instance, let's say Monday? Would anyone notice you're dead before Monday?"

Meaning the day of the referendum vote. Someone doesn't want any bad press. Combine this question with the moat, and there's a bona fide trend here. It's called, *Infernus demon kills ghouls on their way to work.* But to be sure, I need to ask another question. "Ugh, ugh, fire, ugh, ugh, ugh?"

"Come again?" asks Gordon.

I look to Walker pleadingly. He shrugs.

Okay, no help from Walker.

I clear my throat. "I said, ugh, ugh, FIRE, ugh, ugh."

"Still not sure what you mean." Gordon looks to Walker. "Any ideas?"

"Not at all," says my honorary older brother. "Perhaps we should just get to work. We can ask more questions later on."

That's it. My already-short temper is toast. "Are ghouls getting killed on their way to work by Infernus demons?"

You know how you should never yell *fire* in a crowded theater? Turns out, that rule applies to sketchy warehouses and the words *Infernus demons.*

Everyone freaks the fuck out.

"Infernus demon coming!" someone yells.

"Lower the bridge!" calls another ghoul. "Grab your water guns!"

"RUUUUUUUUN!" scream a whole bunch of ghouls in unison.

I look to Walker. "I guess that's a *yes* on the Infernus murder question."

He sets his hand on my shoulder. "Myla-la, you've such a gift for trouble." His all-back eyes glisten with held-in tears of happy.

I rest my palm atop his. "You're welcome."

A mob of terrified ghouls rush past. Walker and I get caught up in the press of bodies. Everyone is heading toward a back wall, where a thin set of planks have been set over the moat. On the other side of the moat, there's a small round pad. The moment ghouls hit that spot, they create portals and disappear.

My brows lift. So that's a portal pad. *Learn something new every day.*

Walker and I follow the rush of ghouls outside, but we bypass the portal pad and march on back to Betsy. Once we get to the car, I find my favorite person wearing body armor and kneeling beside the back door.

It's Lincoln, and he's checking for our trail.

I whip off the ghoul robes and smile my face off. "I thought you were babysitting the Earl?"

"That was the plan," says Lincoln. "But I snuck away under false pretenses."

I mock-pat under my eyes. "Oh wow. that's something I would do." I add in a dramatic sniffle. "I'm a totally bad influence on you."

"Finally," says Walker.

"And most welcome," adds Lincoln.

"So let's take off," I say.

Which is what we do.

Walker drives; Lincoln and I hang in the back. Our destination? The temporary HQ where my parents are scheming out things for Friday.

As we tool along, Walker updates Lincoln on everything we learned today. We all agree that if an Infernus demon is trying to take down Foster Reins, then that's fine with us. The enemy of my enemy is my friend and all that. From there, the chat segues onto parade details.

I try to pay attention, but before I know it, my eyelids become really heavy. And Lincoln is a super-snuggly guy, even when he's wearing body armor. Before I know it, I'm snoring away.

At some point, I'm vaguely aware of Lincoln and Walker discussing how much I need to rest. They change our destination to my ranch house. The next thing I know, Lincoln tucks me under the covers and I sleep like it's my job.

In a way, it is.

8

Next morning, 8 a.m. At this point, I should be thinking about how sweet it is that my parents are getting married. Instead, I can only focus on one phrase, over and over.

Don't look down ... Don't look down ...

People talk about walking on a cloud like it's a good thing. Right now, I'm learning the truth: Clouds suck. How do I know? At this very moment, I stand on a freaking cloud while my parents say their wedding vows a few feet away. It's just me, Mom, Dad, and Verus, the Queen of the Angels who's also conducting the ceremony. Oh, and there's also some angel winging around with a fancy-pants video camera the size of a toilet paper roll.

Angels get all the good tech.

But I digress.

We're on a cloud. And the wedding is both lovely and being live-streamed into every TV set in Purgatory. Plus, I'm wearing my new purple dress. Mom's in a pale purple gown. Dad is in his golden armor with his matching wings on display. Together, my parents are sharing their vows. How I wish I could process what they're saying. But still, all I can focus on is not looking down.

Awkward.

At last, there's a sweet moment where Verus pronounces my parents *man and wife*. They kiss and it's totally sweet. Then—YAY—my escort angels show up again. For the record, these are my favorite people right now. Like Verus, they wear simple white togas with glittery sandals. But their job is to make sure I get off this freaking cloud without ending up a pavement pancake.

The angels in question are Rhiannon and Levi, two of Verus's bodyguards. But honestly? They could be Verus's secret serial killer hit squad and I'd still welcome them with open arms. Because that's what I do right now: stretch my arms wide. Levi and Rhiannon fly closer. Each props one of my arms over their shoulders. Within a few seconds, I'm off the freaking cloud and heading towards the ground again.

"That was lovely," says Levi.

I swallow and keep *not-looking down.*

"Yup," I say in a shaky voice.

For the record, all these two are getting are one-word answers until I hit the ground. At least, my fear of imminent pavement-squashing is lower—not gone, mind you, but lower—so I can focus on other things. Like scrunching my toes so my heels don't fall off and conk someone in the crowd below. Also, there's the whole 'can people see my underwear' question. I'm not usually thong-girl, but it seemed like I needed to do something special for today. So dumb. I'm really regretting that decision now. All I need is for a serious breeze to kick up and my ass cheeks will be all over Purgatory's news. Forever.

"We're almost there," adds Rhiannon.

"Good." Mentally, I know the words 'almost there' mean that I can look down again. Chances are, we are pretty near the ground at this point. That said, the sky remains a very safe place to gaze. Gray clouds. Nothing else. My thoughts collapse into two phrases.

Scrunch toes. Look at the clouds.

At last, my feet hit solid earth once more. With that, my brain starts functioning again. Today's action is right on schedule. As we'd planned, I now stand atop a viewing platform that's a few stories above the main drag of downtown Purgatory. Below me, there stretches your standard parade scene. There's a blocked off street with crowds on either sidewalk. A sense of excitement charges the air.

Nothing's happening. Yet.

Dad lands beside me. He has Mom cradled in his arms and she looks fabulous. Her veil cascades behind her in an arc of lilac. Plus, she's beaming with joy. All thoughts of vertigo and exposed underwear vanish. My parents are married and totally blissed out. This is amazing.

Dad sets Mom on her feet. She pulls me into a deep hug. "Wasn't that lovely?"

"Yes," I say into her shoulder. Mom's a fierce hugger.

Dad taps my shoulder. "I want in on this."

Mom steps back and laughs. A moment later, the three of us are huddle-hugging. Up close, my father looks all cut angles on his handsome face. His cocoa skin positively gleams with all kinds of happy. It's a good day.

But we're not here solely for family time. One thing I'm learning about my mother: She has a natural skill for putting on a show. I guess that's part of what makes her a good politician. You can be kickass at your job, but if you don't let people know about that fact, then you don't get elected.

And Mom *really* wants to become President of Purgatory.

There's a tall microphone stand on our little platform. Mom steps up to the mic. "Greetings, people of Purgatory!"

A massive cheer strikes up from the crowd. Quasis toss purple glitter in the air. It'll be a bitch to clean up, but purple is the color of our realm. Besides, who cares if we're tracking glitter around for a year or two? People hold up signs and shake them for emphasis. I quickly scan some, reading:

Camilla for President

Xavier for First Guy

We Love The Lewises! This last one is even decorated with hand-painted flowers and stuff. Cute!

Mom raises her arms; the crowd falls silent. "You all know it's been a long road for me to this day. At one time, I was the Senator for Diplomacy in Purgatory's old republic. Then I lost my job, my government, and the love of my life, Xavier. For twenty long years, my husband languished in Hell. Now a new future awaits us!"

The crowd cheers their lungs out. Clearly, they love this part. Mom gives the audience a second or two to get the yells out of their system. I make a mental note of how she works her audience. Someday, I hope to be half as good as she is.

Mom continues. "But my history belongs to more than my own family. This is the story of all Purgatory. All of us cherished our lives, history, and purpose … and lost so much in Armageddon's invasion. Alongside myself and my family, every quasi here suffered while outsiders told us what to wear. Which foods we could eat. And how we should spend our work lives. Through it all, our only purpose was to serve our overlords. But now, in this moment, a new future stretches before us. It's exhilarating and frightening at the same time."

I scan the audience. Everyone watches Mom with rapt attention. My heart soars. I've never been prouder to be her daughter.

Reaching over, Mom takes my hand in hers. "If you have ever loved another, then you can imagine the terror that I experienced when I watched my daughter fight Armageddon. She won that battle, but make no mistake. We have more fights before us. Yet we can face these challenges together. We quasis can rebuild our realm, abilities, and faith in each other. So instead of facing this uncertain future with terror, let us trust in each other. And in this way, we can—and will—turn fright into confidence as we celebrate this great adventure."

Mom pauses. No one says a word. That's what you call working a crowd. Mom turns to Dad. "Xavier?"

My father steps up to the microphone. "Greetings!"

Great whoops rise up form the crowd. Dad raises his hands and everyone falls quiet again. "All my life, my family consisted of my fellow archangels. Now I hold every soul in Purgatory deep in my heart. You are my people and future. So in that spirit, I'm proud to say … let the festivities begin!"

Another roar breaks out from the crowd. Dad arches out his wings and leaps off the platform. The wind catches his golden feathers; he sails over the crowd. And indeed, the celebration kicks into high gear.

A wide ribbon of asphalt stretches out before the small tower where Mom and I stand. On the far side of the road, there's a sharp turn. That's where all the parade folks enter the main drag. All along the street, there are cameras to catch every angle and cheer.

Trumpets sound as Lincoln steps out onto the parade route below me. He looks mighty handsome in his princely tunic and crown. Even better, my guy leads a brigade of thrax that ride horses whose manes are woven through with ribbons. Some carry banners. Other thrax rumble out onto the road, this group riding chariots. Another group throws fire swords. Even Walker gets into the act, considering how he's part archangel and all. Mom acts as master of ceremonies, announcing each new marvel from our perch above it all. So cool.

Then, it's my turn.

My mother approaches the microphone once more. "Now, my people! My daughter will display her powers as the Great Scala!"

Mom moves aside. My insides decide that now is a great time to flip-flop around with a vengeance, which sucks. I never became nervous going out before a crowd to kill things, but public speaking?

Hellooooooooo, stage fright.

With trembling steps, I take Mom's place at the microphone. At this moment, I wish there'd been time to tell my parents how my igni have been a little hit-or-miss lately. And now? I have a gagillion eyes locked on me. Plus, my mother's election as president of Purgatory is on the line.

My igni need to show up.

Please, show up.

I clear my throat. "I am the Great Scala. Here are my igni." As speeches go, that was pretty lame. Hopefully, my igni display will make up for things. I raise my right hand and call out to my little glowing buddies.

Nothing happens.

Next I raise my left hand as well. Maybe they need

more of a visual aid about where to show up. The igni sound in my mind, their voices muffled but still present. What the Hell is going on?

Still, not a single lightning bolt appears.

That electric sense of anticipation thickens in the air. This isn't the joy of a great spectacle, though. It's more the shock of watching a car crash.

I raise my arms high and call with all my heart.

I need you, my little ones.

No igni appear. Instead, there's a screech of feedback as someone fiddles with the microphones. Then, below on the parade route, there appears my least favorite person in the after-realms.

Foster Reins.

He's in his space onesie and holding a mic in his hand. I tap the microphone before me. No feedback. No sound. No nothing.

Foster is hijacking the event.

What a creep.

Reins wasn't supposed to do his anti-bastardess stuff until after I showed off my igni and we had some angelic precision flying. But if knowing your moment is a big part of politics, then Foster knows his. There's no better time to interrupt than when his opponent—aka me and my family—are having their one failure of the day.

My igni.

I step back from the microphone. If nothing else, I can make this look like it's part of the show. Inside, I'm screaming one word, over and over.

Fuuuuuuuuuuuck.

The speakers blare the Stellar One theme song. The crowd starts dancing. Fresh signs appear.

Foster for President

Commander Starling for Purgatory

The Future is Foster

Maybe it's just me, but it feels like the cheering is louder and longer than it was for my family. A weight of worry settles into my bones. This day is going off the rails.

"My people!" calls Foster. "Who wants to reach the future with a proven candidate?"

The crowd cheers. I boo.

"And now, let's acknowledge the phenomenal power of the Great Scala. How about that igni show, huh?" There's barely a sound as Foster fake-claps with his microphone in one hand. The guy is such a poser. He's not celebrating me. Nope, Foster is only highlighting my failure to conjure a single lightning bolt. Which is why no one is clapping but him.

Total dick move.

"Now, now," chides Foster. "You can cheer better than that. Let's hear it for the Great Scala, who is finally no longer a bastardess!"

At this, the crowd goes nutso. Rage twists through my limbs. What a nightmare. Standing on a stage with my parents and being called a bastardess. Narrowing my eyes, I purse my lips and blow Foster a little thing I like to call, *the kiss of death.*

Your turn is coming, Mr. Reins.

Not sure how it will happen, but I'll figure out something.

Foster turns to the opposite side of the parade route. "And now, to celebrate the Scala's legitimacy, let's welcome the Stellar One parade!"

I stifle the urge to roll my eyes. How does a Stellar One parade celebrate me in any way, shape or form? This is all about Foster Reins. Again. To make things worse, I can't help but notice that new beer and hotdog vendors are now circulating through the crowds. It's *all you can eat* free food and drink with the Foster Reins logo on it.

Damn. I wish we'd thought of that.

The Stellar One music gets cranked up to an ear-splitting volume as his parade begins. Row after row of little kids march down the street, all of them in Havoc costumes. Much as I hate to admit it, this is a good move as well. The Havoc are ideal dress-up for kids. Based on how many children Foster has recruited here, I'd say half the crowd has a little relative who's marching right now.

Crap. This guy is gooooood.

For a few minutes, there's nothing but cheering crowds and the scent of roasting hot dogs. Lights flash as parents take pictures of their children in Havoc costumes. The crowd cheers as a pick-up truck covered in Foster logos hauls a tall metal trailer onto the street.

My brows lift. Ah-ha. I've seen that particular trailer before, back at the warehouse. It's the one with a not-a-fireworks display inside. Whatever lies hidden inside, Foster already pushed things over the top with the kiddie display and free beer. My heart sinks. Foster is winning the day.

Then a great roar breaks the air.

"GRRRRR!"

Every cell in my body goes on alert. That cry has nothing to do with Stellar One. Nothing else cries with that particular mixture of screech and growl.

A demon is bellowing its lungs out. And based on the sound, it's not coming from inside the trailer but from about a quarter mile away. What the WHAT?

I scan Foster's face. He looks as shocked as I feel.

Which means one thing. This big bad isn't part of the Stellar One show. And there are hundreds of little kids waiting on the streets, wearing the absolute worst camouflage ever.

Oh, fuck fuck fuckity FUCK fuck.

9

"GRRROWL!"

Another roar breaks the morning air. This time, it's one of those deep howls that go straight down your spine. The crowd falls silent. Leaning over the railing on our podium, I scan the street. Far below, some ghoul grandpa grabs Foster's elbow. I can't hear the question from the older quasi, but Foster gives his reply right into the microphone.

"No, this isn't part of the show," says Foster.

When in battle, fear can be an almost visible thing. After those words from Foster, ripples of terror sweep across the crowd. The temperature seems to drop.

"GRRROWL!"

Yet another cry sounds. The scent of charcoal carries in the air. My gaze locks onto the tall bureau style container that was dragged onto the street. A memory appears from Lincoln back in Lady Midnight's dressing room.

No one cares about the sparkles, they all want what's inside.

My eyes widen. Now, I know exactly what's in that thing. And why we're in trouble. My gaze catches Lincoln's. He stands at the base of the platform. We share a slow nod. There's no need for long explanations. I know he realizes the danger here, same as I do.

"Run!" screams Foster. "Run or die!"

On reflex, I step up to the microphone on our platform. "Do not move."

In response, everyone moves. The crowd surges as folks race to a little place called *not here.*

Raising my arms, I call for my igni one last time. At first, there is only silence.

Then, they heed my summons at last.

Millions of tiny lightning bolts instantly materialize. The street, the sky, the little kiddos in their costumes … everyone becomes surrounded by the tiny bolts of power. Even better, these are the light igni, the ones who send souls to Heaven. They give off a naturally calming vibe.

"I'm here with you," I say into the mic. "My igni are

here. No one will hurt you. But you need to stay quiet and stand still." Surprisingly enough, the crowd seems to heed me this time. the press of bodies stops. I turn to my parents, ready to explain my plan.

But Mom seems to guess it already. Leaning in, she kisses my cheek. "Go get them, baby."

Dad winks. "Same here."

"You know what this is, right?" I ask. After all, Dad is the demon expert in my life.

"Whatever it is," says Dad smoothly. "You're the one to fix it."

My heart swells with all kinds of pride. Grinning, I kick off my shoes. After hoisting myself over the side of the platform, I scale down the scaffolding that leads to the street below. Lincoln stands there at the base of the makeshift tower. Seeing him gives me another jolt of confidence.

We can do this.

"How long do we have?" I ask. There's no need to add the part about *'until the big bad demon arrives?'*

"Any second now."

Foster's voice echoes through the air. "No one knows trouble better than I do. Who faced down the Havoc's evil three-headed queen? Which starship navigated the Gauntlet of Danger not once, but twice? I told the Great Scala to have everyone stand still. You know why?

Because this is *really* all part of *my* show. We planned it out beforehand. And you know what that means: the Great Scala herself admits that I know how to handle any kind of trouble, even when it's all totally for show and no one is in any real danger."

I roll my eyes for real this time. *What a loser.* I can't believe that Foster's trying to turn this to his advantage. I scan the crowd. Speaking of Commander Creep, there's no sign of Foster. I look to Lincoln. "Where is that guy?"

Lincoln inspects the same sea of faces and inhales deeply. I have no idea what my guy is really detecting, but I also have no doubt of one fact.

Lincoln will find Foster, easy peasy.

Sure enough, my guy takes off into the crowd. I keep pace as we dodge around knots of terrified people. Fortunately, everyone keeps standing in place. It doesn't hurt that the igni are still swimming around the air, giving everyone something pleasant to focus on.

Within seconds, we find Foster. The ghoul is crouched beside his massive trailer thingy. The microphone remains gripped in his fist. "I'm the real demon hunting expert here," says Foster into the mic. "And you'll see this for certain any moment now."

I reach out my hand toward Foster. The ghoul shakes

his head quickly. "I'm fine down here," he says in a shaky voice.

My mind takes a snapshot of this moment. There's a big bad demon about to show up and Foster spends his time hiding out while singing his own praises. Total douchebag.

"I wasn't offering you help you up," I explain. "Hand over the microphone."

Foster's all black eyes widen. Yet he does not loosening his grip on this mic. At all.

Another roar sounds. This one is closer than ever. Foster pulls the microphone so close to his lips, it's like he's licking the thing. I lean over, ready to wrestle the mic free. My tail does the tough work, though. It sucker punches Foster right in the gut. He gasps and drops the mic ... which I catch before it hits the ground.

"Nice work, boy." I pat my tail's end.

A moment ago, Foster was a groveling loser who crouched behind a tall trailer. Now, he's a man with a mission I like to call, *Mister Terrible Wants His Microphone Back*. In other words, Foster leaps to his feet and makes grabby hands in my direction.

Fast as a whip, Lincoln pulls out his baculum, ignites the rods as a long sword, and points the fiery blade right at Foster's throat. "Not another word," says my guy.

When Lincoln wants to, he can pack a lot of menace into just one syllable. And I just counted five right there.

In fact, I've never seen my guy angrier than he is now. Foster makes actual 'eep eep eep' noises while he goes back into his crouch by the trailer.

With Foster in his place, Lincoln turns to me. "You got this?"

Foster rises again. "You can not take this day away from me. Give back that microphone. Start up the parade again."

Lincoln tilts his head. "On second thought …" He extinguishes his baculum, winds up his right fist, and punches Foster straight in the jaw. The ghoul falls over, unconscious. I must say, the thud of Foster hitting the pavement is an especially satisfying sound.

With Foster out, Lincoln then returns his attention to me. "Changed my mind. Hanging with you will be more fun."

"So true. Give me a leg up?"

Lincoln laces his fingers together, giving me a foothold. I step onto his hands. A moment later, I'm standing atop the trailer. Lincoln follows. Thousands of faces still stare in my direction. I notice a lot of wide eyes and twitchy expressions. My people are terrified, but they're staying put.

So far, so good.

For a moment, I hear the childlike voices of my igni in my mind. Then, those tones fade. It's as if my little ones are being yanked away for some reason.

With a burst of light, all my igni vanish.

Oh, crud. I'd blame the ghouls for my lack of igni, but there are bigger problems to deal with right now. Namely, the loss of igni is not a big winner with the crowd. People gasp. Others weep. More inch toward the exits. A baby cries its head off.

I tap the mic. "Attention, everybody." The crowd turns in my direction. "I need you to stay calm and stand absolutely still. Unlike certain lying liars, I actually know my demons. Everyone will be totally fine. Just do what I tell you." I then pat my tail. "Go to it, bud."

With a flourish, my tail punches through the roof of the metal box. With my tail keeping a firm grip in the metal, I walk across the top of the trailer. Beneath me, the structure rumbles. I smile. As I suspected, there are no fireworks inside this thing.

Foster is hiding other surprises.

Across the street, a massive bear made from red flame steps into the center of the street. The Infernus demon. It sniffs toward the little Havoc kids and chuffs. This isn't a growl of anger. It's fear.

"Hey, Momma Bear," I state into the mic. "They're in here."

Lincoln ignites his baculum into a fiery net that tumbles into the belly of the trailer. "Got one." Lincoln hauls up the line. The net comes atop the trailer and with it? A newborn bear cub made of crimson fire. The little guy sees his mother, rears on his back legs and lets out a yelp. Poor guy.

I speak into the microphone again. "Listen to me, kids. Slowly step out of the Momma Bear's way. She doesn't want to hurt anyone. She just wants her cubs."

The costumed children carefully move of the Infernus demon's way. The Momma Fire Bear lumber-runs down the pavement, heading right in our direction. Behind her, she leaves a trail of charred paw prints in the pavement. It's the same path I saw in the forest after returning from Antrum.

Meanwhile, Lincoln hauls the second cub out of the trailer. Along with its sibling, this one is crazy tiny, reminding me more of a kitten than a bears. For her part, Momma Fire Bear lumbers up to the trailer, scoops her babies from the roof, and settles down with them in her lap.

I speak into the microphone once more. "You see, Infernus demons are rarely aggressive. This one was only protecting her cubs. Someone—and by *someone* I mean Foster Reins—lured her out of her den. From there, it was easy to pick up these newborns. Foster's goal is pretty clear. He wanted to prove to you all that he knows demon stuff as well as me, my family, and my—" I look to Lincoln, at a loss for words.

My guy leans into the microphone. "Her boyfriend, Prince Lincoln."

I grin. "Yes, that. Momma Fire Bear could scent her cubs. If you'd tried to run, it would have set off her predator instincts. The best thing to do with bears, whether mortal or demonic, is to stay still. Now that she has her cubs, Momma Fire Bear will be fine."

Sure enough, Momma Fire Bear carries her cubs with her right front paw while she hobble-crawls away from the crowd. Before she disappears from view, Momma Fire Bear stands on her hind legs and lets out a roar. This time, the tone holds no fury. Only gratitude.

Lincoln laces his fingers with mine. "Well done."

A blush colors my face. "Thank you."

There's an expectant something-something in my soul. It's the sensation you have when you leave a room and know you left something in the kitchen on. Only in this case, it isn't that I forgot to close the fridge. Nope. That nagging feeling is because thousands of quasis are still staring at me. And those are just the ones lining the parade route. How many more saw this whole thing on television?

I clear my throat and address the crowd. "So, I'm

super proud of you guys. We all aced that like a team." I scan the parade route and sigh. "This whole thing got out of hand, and that's partly my fault. I thought we needed to out-do Foster in terms of impressing you with a big show. But in the end, running a realm isn't about any razzle dazzle. It's about one question: when trouble comes, who holds your trust? Which folks will have your back and fight for your future? You know where my family and I stand. We'll protect you because that's what we do. Guard. Help. Lead. If you vote for my mother on Monday, both my parents will work their asses off for your future. And so will I. Together, we will take our realm back."

Over on the podium, Mom and Dad launch into a speech about their plans for Purgatory I feel a little wobbly on my bare feet. Lincoln eyes me closely. "Are you all right?" he asks.

"Mmmm." I screw my mouth up onto one side of my face. "Not really."

Lincoln runs his finger along my jawline. "You're still recovering from that fight with Armageddon." Without another word, he scoops me into his arms. Nearby, everyone cheers. It seems they're taking this as a romantic move from my now-official boyfriend versus the fact that I'm freaking exhausted. Stupid Armageddon.

I lean into Lincoln's shoulder as he leaps down from atop the trailer and strides through the crowd. In short order, I fall asleep. I'm vaguely aware of Lincoln finding Walker, who opens a portal that gets me home. Once in my bedroom, I kick off my gown, slip on a nightshirt, and slip under the covers. Lincoln tucks me in and I tumble into a deep sleep.

Who knew that not-fighting demons could wipe a girl out?

For the next few days, I spend tons of quality time asleep. And in a strange twist of awesomeness, my worshippers take a holiday. As in, there's no one outside my window, singing spirituals or asking for armpit tattoos.

Not sure how this miracle happened, but I'll take it.

One downside: My dreams go back to being hella boring. That said, I don't dream about Commander Starling, which is a good thing. All the sprinkles have definitely fallen off the Stellar One sundae, if you know what I mean.

At some point, it's Monday night. Returns are coming in from the election, and we're all hanging out in the living room. And by 'all,' I mean myself, Mom, Dad, Walker and Lincoln. The little black and white TV has been relocated from the kitchen. Now, we're all chilling in the living room, watching the Greek announce a rolling tally of voting results. Over the past few hours, I've eaten my weight in demon bars. By this point, the sugar high is so intense, it's like my teeth are vibrating out of my skull.

Lincoln, Walker and I lounge on the couch. My parents keep pacing along the opposite side of the room. Every so often, they pause behind us, inspect the results on TV, and then go back to pacing. Just watching them is exhausting. Maybe it's a sugar crash, but I'm starting to feel sleepy again.

The grainy screen moves in for a close-up on the Greek. The old ghoul looks especially long-jowled today. I take that as a good sign. The voting results have been in Mom's favor all night, so the Greek is bummed because he might be out of a job soon.

There's only one final precinct left to report in.

On screen, the Greek raises a pile of papers before him. "We have news. The results have come in from the Purgatory Isles. The vote is for self rule by 78% and for President Lewis by 82%." He huffs out a long breath. "Congratulations, quasi people. You now have home rule. As Pericles said, *what you leave behind is not what is engraved in stone monuments, but what is woven into the lives of others.*"

Whatever. The Greek can quote dead guys while he packs his bags.

Back in my living room, everyone jumps to stand. There's a ton of cheering, back slaps and kisses. My tail gets into the act, giving out high fives. On the TV, the Greek steps aside to allow another ghoul to step into the frame.

Foster Reins.

"And what do you have to say?" asks the Greek.

The Greek shoves the oversized microphone in Foster's face. "Greetings, people of Purgatory," says Foster in a monotone. "I am here to give my concession speech to Camilla Lewis, who I'm sure will be an okay President."

Lincoln and I share a sly smile. "Looks like Foster has a little bruise action going on his jawline," I point out.

My guy winks. "Wonder how that happened."

I snap my fingers, as if a memory were just appearing. "I got it. Maybe that happened when you kicked his ass."

Back on the television, the Greek turns to Foster once more. "And what about you?" asks the host. "What are your plans?"

"The Oligarchy have given me a plum assignment guarding the Towers of Sanctity."

The Greek frowns. "Seriously?"

"Guarding the Towers of Sanctity." Walker hisses in a breath through his teeth. "That's code for acting as personal servant to the Oligarchy. And when I say personal, you think, *no fun.*"

I sniff. "Couldn't happen to a better guy."

Back on screen, Foster keeps going. "The Oligarchy have also asked me to relay a message to you all. The Great Scala's powers are weakening."

That gets my attention. I stop giving out high fives and stare at the screen. A chill of worry creeps up my back.

"Is that still happening, honey?" asks Mom.

"They've been a little on the fritz," I allow. "But my abilities are all new. I figured it would just work itself out." I close my eyes tightly. "I summon thee, oh igni."

Nothing. Not even little voices in my head.

This is so *not good.*

A wild look takes over Foster's all-black eyes. "The ghouls have planted Lucifer's Orb in Purgatory! With every mile the orb moved closer to your lands, Myla's powers lessened. Now, she can only move souls to Hell. Purgatory stores millions of souls for processing. Unless all those innocents go to Hell, the many spirits you hold will all break free. Angry ghosts will overrun your lands. Do you hear me, Myla? Send them to Hell or else!"

For a long moment, all I can see is Foster's crazed face on television, telling me that my powers are limited. And escaping spirits are no joke. It's happened before. A total bloodbath.

In the back of my mind, I'm aware that someone's hugging me. Sense returns to my mind as I find Lincoln holding me close. Meanwhile, another someone is on the phone screaming at the television station. As my mind clears, I realize that's my mother.

"I'm not your President right now, but I will be. Get that man off the air!" She slams down the receiver. "They won't listen."

Walker opens a ghoul portal. "I got this," he says in his deep voice.

On our living room floor, Walker opens a dark rectangle. A moment later, Walker appears on our small black and white television screen. Raising his fist, Walker punches Foster on the unmarked side of his face. The ghoul drops like a wet sack of trash. Walker glares down at the unconscious Foster. "That's for hurting my Myla-la."

There's a long pause where I think everyone in Purgatory just gasped. I mean, people noticed Walker hanging around my family, but they never knew he'd portal into a TV studio and punch Foster Reins in the face for us.

The Greek turns to the camera once more. "Well, folks. There you have it. Purgatory now has home rule and a new president, Camilla Lewis. This is the Greek, signing off."

The screen goes dark. There's a moment that lasts a million years where the four of us just stare at the blank screen. Dad is the first to break the silence.

"Is this how things usually go around here?" he asks.

"What do you mean?" I ask. "How what starts off as a quiet wedding turns into a massive parade and anti-bastardess event … which then is raided by an angry fire bear who wants her cubs … which helps us us win the election … only to have the Oligarchy leave behind something called Lucifer's Orb … prompting Walker to go on live television and punch a popular ghoul celebrity in the face?"

Mom sniffs. "I don't think Foster is all that popular any more."

Dad nods. "I agree on that point, Cam." My father focuses on me. "But the rest of it. That's exactly what I meant."

"Oh, yeah. That's pretty much my life." I turn to Lincoln. "Wouldn't you say?"

My guy beams. "I would say. And I couldn't be happier about it."

And you know what's awesome? He totally means it.

Dad straightens the lapels of his gray suit. "In the spirit of our new family dynamic, I should like to announce another momentous event for today."

"Really?" I ask.

"Yes." Dad's face gets all serious, which is what I consider his *General Of The Angels* look. He turns to Mom. "I have a confession to make."

Mom narrows her eyes. "What is it?"

"I've been sneaking around lately," answers Dad.

"You have?" I ask.

For some reason, I could handle all the other strangeness over the past week without too much freaking out. Fire bear? I'm all over that. Finding a purple dress? Not too much of an issue. But the fact that Foster Reins was actually right and that my father was really sneaking around? That has my heart rate speeding.

Dad rubs his palms together. "Let's all load into Betsy and I'll show you."

A chorus of half-hearted 'okay's' fills the air. I grab Lincoln's hand like it's a lifeline. With that, we all head out and load into a POS station wagon.

This better not suck.

inutes later, the four of us are tooling around Purgatory: Mom, Dad, Lincoln and me. It doesn't take long for one fact to become crystal clear.

Dad drives like a nutjob.

To my father, red lights are suggestions more than rules. And turns? I swear, Dad is trying to bust a tire. Mom rides shotgun, and she's gripping the dashboard like her life depends on it. I'm in the back seat, trying not to barf. Lincoln thinks it's a hoot. Every time we take a hard turn, Mom and I get smashed into the car window like bugs. Lincoln somehow stays upright and beams.

After a while, Mom asks the question. "How much

farther, Xav?" I know that tone from my Mother. She's about two minutes away from taking over driving duty.

"Just a few more minutes," says Dad casually.

SCREECH!

My father takes another turn at high speed. Lincoln chuckles. I feel sick to my stomach.

"Did you know," begins Dad. "This is an original model Satan's Traveller 600, which has an eight cylinder engine and magic propulsion?"

My jaw falls open with shock. A realization hits me. "You're a car guy."

"Oh, yeah," says Mom. "Back in the day, your father's favorite spot was always the diplomatic travel pool."

"Pool?" asks Lincoln.

"It's a big garage where they store all the vehicles for official use," explains Dad. "The diplomat plates mean you can't get a ticket, no matter what you do."

SCREECH!

Another high-speed turn follows. Someone in a rusted pick-up lies on their horn. Dad laughs. Clearly, my father is having the time of his life. Sure, I'm still feeling nauseous, but I can't find it in me to rain on his vehicular parade.

"A few items to discuss on this mission," says Dad. He's definitely back in his Angelic General Mode now.

"I'm sure you all suspected that once your Mother became President, we'd need a new residence.

"Sure," I say. In all honesty, living conditions was one of those foggy ideas that I knew might happen at some point. However, it's not like I spent hours thumbing through issues of *Architectural Purgatory* or anything.

Dad pulls up before a very tall and pokey fence. It's the kind that's made from a twisty black iron bars. In this case, those rods are melted into the shapes of ghoul silhouettes. I scan the street. We're in Upper Purgatory. This is ghoul central.

My father gestures toward the windshield. "Beyond this fence, there's a house that was recently abandoned by a wealthy ghoul collective."

That perks my interest. "As in, they ran away after I kicked Armageddon out of Purgatory?"

Dad turns to look into the back seat. "You got it. They were in charge of the library system for Purgatory."

"So they suck," I deadpan. The library ghouls raided all the bookstores and repositories in our realm. After that, those undeadlies sold off everything and then replaced it with classic titles like *I Love Ghouls* and *How to Please Your New Overlords*.

Mom sniffs. "Let's just say they had every reason to believe they'd be safer somewhere else."

"Let's get a better look-see," says Dad.

And with that, I realize one key fact. In a matter of weeks, my father has gone from Hell survivor and angelic warrior ... into full father, including doing semi-embarrassing stuff like using *look-see* in a sentence.

I glance over to Lincoln, wince and mouth one word: "Dads."

Lincoln winks and whispers on word in reply: "Aldred."

And with that, I know exactly what my guy means. We both have parental issues. It's cool. I scooch over so I can lean against Lincoln's side. Being near him is the best.

Dad taps the horn. The wall-like gate splits in two, revealing a winding driveway. The first thing I notice is that the road winds through a lawn made of actual green grass. We just don't get that in Purgatory. First of all, it's next to impossible to coax anything green to grow here. And second, whenever greenery existed, the ghouls tore it up to make worm farms.

But this place? There's a rich emerald lawn that's like something out of a human television show. Not Stellar One, of course. The Brady Bunch, maybe.

We drive up a windy road toward nothing less than a Goth mega mansion. There are tons of pointy roofs, wooden turrets, and heavy shutters. Dozens of quasis mill around outside. They're busy doing stuff like planting flowers. Watering the lawn. Painting the black wooden exterior even more black. I recognize these faces.

My worshippers. They're all here.

Truth time. I did not see that one coming.

Dad parks in the round driveway that loops past the main entrance. The moment takes on a surreal edge. My father just said we'd need a real house once Mom was President. Is this our new home?

The four of us slide out of the car. For the first time, I notice a ghoul standing by a group of quasis setting up their gardening stuff. The figure turns and it's Walker.

I grin. Of course, it's Walker.

My honorary older brother comes over to say his hellos. We mill around the front of the house, soaking in its massive Goth awesomeness. Walker moves to stand beside me and Lincoln.

"What do you think?" asks my honorary brother. At this point, the phrase shit-eating grin perfectly captures the look on Walker's face.

"That you're an awesome liar," I deadpan.

Walker blinks innocently. "Whatever do you mean?"

"You said my worshippers were lured away by a fake Myla."

"Fake Myla," repeats Lincoln. He shakes his head. "Only you, Walker."

"About that." Walker taps his lips dramatically. "Actually, it was the real Myla that inspired your worshippers to relocate. Those folks were only hanging around your home because they wanted to help you. I just gave them a little more direction."

Going up on tiptoe, I kiss Walker's cheek. "Thanks for stepping in. I guess I was just so surprised at having worshippers, I didn't really think things through."

Lincoln matches Walker's sneaky face with one of his own. "Imagine what all these people could do with even more focus," says my guy.

Walker mock-gasps with surprise. "You don't say?"

"Hey now." I set my fists on my hips. "Have you two already been scheming how to fix stuff after Mom became president?"

"Me?" Walker works up a look of fake shock. "Why, the thought may have occurred to me once or twice. For instance, those towers you use for ghost storage are incredibly inefficient."

"I heard that." Mom points right at Walker. "You just got a job running infrastructure, among other things."

Walker bows slightly. "I'm honored."

For the record, I love the direction this conversation is taking. "And can you give me a crash course on those towers while you're at it? I need to learn all that stuff and fast."

"Of course," intones Walker.

Dad paces before the house in a quick rhythm. It's like watching a puppy with a treat. "The place is incredibly high-tech inside. Lots of stainless steel and gadgets. Plus, it's all ours. Want to take a look?"

Mom takes his hand. "Love to."

Mom, Dad and Walker speed up the steps. Lincoln and I start to follow when someone taps my shoulder. Turning, I find myself face to face with tracksuit grandma.

"Oh, hello," I say. It's an effort not to make my 'eek' face. Inside my heart, I think two words: *shields up.* This could get nasty.

"I've decided you're okay," she says. "That speech you gave about us working together. It was the bee's knees."

I figure that insect stuff is old lady talk for 'you did a good job.' So I smile. "Thank you."

"And you don't even have to sign my armpit. Our relationship is better without it, I think."

I grin. "Thanks for moving past that."

Tracksuit grandma offers me her fist to bump. My tail does the bumping because it loves any chance at attention. And with that, tracksuit grandma takes off.

No requests or singing. It's pretty amazing, as a matter of fact.

Lincoln gives my hand a gentle squeeze. Together, we step toward the front door. The thought hits me. In this moment, I have my home and it's not just a physical place. It's wherever I find Lincoln, Walker and my parents. Sure, my powers are blocked right now, and that situation could release a million bloodthirsty ghosts onto the street (because no way am I sending innocents to Hell). But with my family nearby, trouble better watch out.

There's a good chance we'll all kick some ass.

—The End—

The adventure continues in our fourth story, Sharkie and Snickerdoodles!

FOUR. HERBIE AND BABY HOTDOGS

Introduction From the Author, Christina Bauer

Dear reader,

This story takes place *after* the events of *Scala*, which is the second book in the Angelbound Origins series. Having finished their wedding adventures, Myla and Lincoln visit the Ryder mansion to uncover dark secrets regarding the evil Earl of Acca.

I hope you enjoy *Herbie and Baby Hotdogs!*

Sincerely,

CB

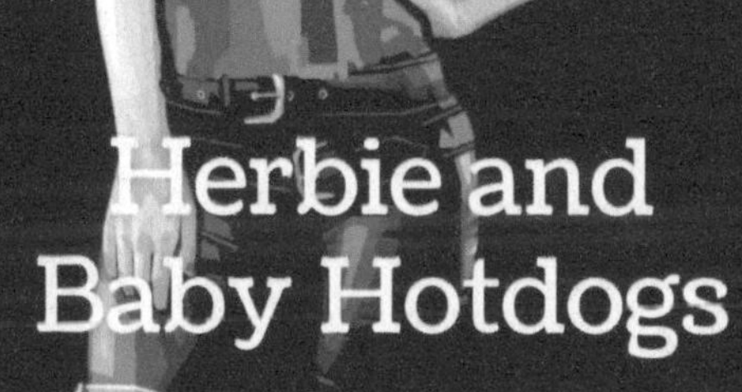

Herbie and Baby Hotdogs

*L*incoln and I stroll up the round drive to the Ryder mansion. Most of the time, my guy and I are either fighting *big bads*, kissing like crazy, or stuck spending time apart. Sharing a quiet walk like this one? Major treat.

I soak in the moment.

Grey skies arch overhead. Early morning dew glistens on the mansion's white wooden exterior. More condensation drips off the emerald shrubs encircling the building's base. The scent of cut grass fills the air.

Life is good.

We pause before the front door. Normally, my guy and I are bombarded by now, mostly from quasis who want me to bless their goldfish or something. But it's early a.m. and the mansion grounds are deserted. I give my guy the once-over, simply because I can. Lincoln's in casual mode today, meaning he sports a black t-shirt, jeans and hefty boots. Meanwhile, I wear my white Scala robes and carry a leather satchel.

Key fact: In the past, you could never get decent handbags in Purgatory. Then I kicked the ghouls out and local shopping got crazy-better. Total victory bonus.

I ring the doorbell. Recently, the Ryders installed a fancy number that bongs to the tune of *Some Enchanted Evening.* It's an odd choice, but the Ryders are all part lust demon. To them, using a hookup song as a doorbell makes sense. Seconds pass before a muffled voice sounds behind the wooden panel.

"Who goes there?"

Lincoln gives me the side-eye. "Is that … Zeke?"

"Yup." On reflex, I pop the P-sound on the word's end.

This sucks.

Here's the deal. Cissy promised Zeke wouldn't be around this morning. Sure, Lincoln is my fiancée, but it's not like we've known each other for years. Plus, there's already plenty of weirdness in my life: I'm a demi-goddess, Dad's an archangel, and Mom's President of Purgatory. And that list doesn't even leave my immediate family. I'm in no rush to introduce my guy into my larger circle of strangeness.

Which mostly includes Zeke.

"Answer my question. Who goes there? I'm the Captain of the President's Guard."

"Maybe," I correct. "Mom's *considering* it."

Which is true. That said, Mom will probably give Zeke the gig. Two reasons. First, Zeke stood by my mother when she faced Armageddon. Loyalty like that gets rewarded. Second, my bestie Cissy is killing it in the diplomacy department. That's a huge help to the government in general, and to my mother in particular. There's a catch, though. Cissy's dating Zeke, who wants in on the military. Hence the guard thing.

I jingle the handle. "Open the door. We're late for Cissy."

"I need proof of identity," states Zeke. "Give me the password."

"Are you serious?" I throw up my hands. "No one told me you were guarding the door, let alone asking for passwords."

Beside me, Lincoln toys with the hilt of his baculum. "Shall I ignite my long sword?" His eyes light up with a sly gleam. "It would slice through this wood like butter."

"I heard that!" calls Zeke. "You didn't say anyone was with you, Myla."

I look to Lincoln. "Please don't ruin the door. Zeke's mom will call my mother in a nanosecond. Nothing but hideousness will result, trust me." I jiggle the handle harder while yelling at the door. "Listen to yourself, Captain Man Candy! You just called me Myla. You know who I am. And I distinctly used the word 'we' when I said—and I quote—*we're late for Cissy.* So obviously, someone's with me. Now open up already."

A drumroll of footsteps sounds from inside the house. At last, the door swings open. Inside the threshold, there stands Zeke in full purple body armor, complete with the crest of Purgatory's New Republic on his bicep. Beside him stands a very red-faced Cissy in a purple skirt suit. She's panting. No doubt, my bestie sprinted to the door.

"I'm so sorry," says Cissy. To emphasize her worry, she wrings her hands. On anyone else, that move would look totally fake, but my bestie sells it like a pro. That's why she's so good at the diplomacy thing.

"It's fine," I say. *And it is.* Cissy's working her ass off these days. Incredibly sweet of her to come by early just so Lincoln and I can bypass my worshippers. Sure, Walker gives my followers little projects to stay out of my hair, but Purgatory's a massive place. There's always someone who doesn't get the memo, if you know what I mean.

Lincoln nods regally. "Greetings."

"Hey, Lincoln." Cissy turns to Zeke and freezes. She looks him over from head to toe. Twice. It's as if she's seeing her boyfriend for the first time this morning. Which is probably the case.

"You're wearing body armor today," says Cissy.

Zeke puffs out his chest. "It just came in. Official guard armor. Thought I'd try it on and practice, you know?"

I raise my hand. "True story. Zeke was being totally annoying at the door. For the record, there's no password system here."

Cissy and Zeke ignore me because that's what they do sometimes. Zeke arches his right brow. It's what Cissy calls his 'delicious' look. He then gestures across his body armor. "What do you think?"

A long pause follows while Cissy says nothing. My bestie is like me in one respect. Both of us love ourselves a man in body armor. Cissy has dropped all pretense of hand-wringing and has segued completely into guy-ogling.

"I like it." Cissy drags out the word *like* for like five seconds.

I clear my throat. "Cis."

My bestie doesn't even look in my direction. "Hmm?"

"We're supposed to meet that Hanner guy," I remind her.

Cissy stays in eye-lock with Zeke. "His name's Herbie."

"Right." I make *twiddle fingers* at her and Zeke. "So the first step in the process is for the two of you to move backward so Lincoln and I can enter the mansion."

"What?" Cissy blinks hard. "Oh, right."

Together, Cissy and Zeke retreat into the reception area. Then they start ogling each other some more. Zeke's eyes flare red. That means his lust demon is active.

Yipes.

There are some memories that are so disturbing, I'd like to burn them out of my brain. Many of them involve Cissy and Zeke making out. Even thinking about it makes me shiver. Next my tail gets into the act. It arches over my shoulder to point at my face. The arrowhead end wags from side to side, meaning *no, no, no.*

I couldn't agree more.

Grasping Lincoln's wrist, I yank him into the building, through reception and then straight down the hallway leading to the diplomatic wing. As we speed away, I call over my shoulder. "I know where, uh," *what's that name again?* It's too stressful right now to remember, so I take a wild guess. "I can find Hanford on my own so … buh-bye!"

Lincoln narrows his eyes into what I call his *contemplative face*. This happens a lot when he asks me questions about quasi life. "I thought you were part lust demon."

Suddenly I realize how I've lost some cool factor here. The Cissy-Zeke thing freaked me out. Releasing my vise-like grasp on Lincoln's wrist, I force a more leisurely sashay-style pace down the hallway. "What do you mean?" I ask, very casually and with the utmost level of awesome possible. Maybe.

"Cissy and Zeke are about to kiss," says Lincoln.

"Eew."

"And there's my question. Why would that be upsetting?"

Stopping, I fix Lincoln with my most serious stare. "Two words: spit strings." I hold up my palms so they're about three feet apart. "Of like, epic proportions." Okay, that was six words, but hopefully my guy will get the idea.

And does he ever.

Lincoln's face contorts into a look that can only be described as, *disgusted*. Little lines form between his eyebrows and everything. "You are a goddess among women," he states solemnly. "Thank you for sparing me that sight."

At this point, it's worth noting that Lincoln did not even wince when we exploded Simia demons the other week. There were blue guts in our hair and everything. Therefore I find his reaction to the *spit string* situation to be totally validating.

"You're welcome." I grin. "Now let's go talk to, uh, Hector."

"It's Herbie."

My guy and the names. He's a wizard when it comes to memory. Which is one of many reasons why I'm glad Lincoln's here today. My eyes widen. In all the excitement between Zeke and Cissy, I've gotten distracted from the real purpose of our visit.

Meeting a key witness.

Getting evidence against Acca.

Then using said facts to lock Aldred up in his *forever-jail.*

Oh, yeeeeeeeeeah.

A few minutes later, Lincoln and I stand before another closed door. This time, it leads to a chamber in the diplomatic wing of the Ryder mansion. I knock gently.

"Who is it?" The voice is young, male and decidedly shaky. Must be Herbie.

"It's Myla Lewis."

"Who?!" A crash sounds through the door as Herbie knocks something over.

Yipes. I keep forgetting how no one connects my real identity with my deity alter-ego. "I mean, it's the Great Scala."

"Oh," says Herbie. "Come in, please."

I push open the door to witness one of the most unexpected sights ever. A scrawny teenager sits at a massive oak table surrounded by empty chairs. *Herbie.* The kid's got a long nose, spikey brown hair, huge brown eyes and a T-shirt that reads 'I heart the Human Channel.' But that's not the surprising part. Nope. What's an eye opener is how white ceramic bowls cover the tabletop. And all those containers are filled with tiny yet disgusting food items.

Ick. And I thought the spit strings were bad.

Lincoln steps in beside me. "Greetings."

"Who are you?" Herbie cranes his neck. "You don't have a tail."

"He's my fiancée," I explain.

Herbie scrunches up his face, as if contemplating this news very carefully. "And you're the Great Scala."

I shoot him a thumbs-up. "Bingo."

Herbie shrugs. "Then I guess it's okay then." He pulls a fresh bowl closer. "You don't kind if I eat, do you?"

I make shoo fingers at him and try not to look too closely. "Nope. Knock yourself out."

Lincoln makes his *contemplative* face again. "What are you eating there, Herbie?"

"Baby hot dogs. Want one?"

I stifle the urge to barf. "No." In my mind, that word came out all low and smooth. But based on how everyone is staring at me with wide eyes? I might have screamed it a bit.

Herbie grabs his baby hotdog bowl and scooches back his chair. "Maybe I should leave."

"No, please." I take the seat across from Herbie and try to ignore the twenty-odd bowls filled with baby hot dogs. "Here's the deal. I had an awful baby hotdog incident in the second grade at Purgatory Prep." I set my hand on my heart. "True story."

"I'm listening." Herbie pops another baby hotdog into his mouth. I really wish he'd use utensils, but I'm in no position to make demands right now. I need Herbie giving evidence more than I want sanitary eating practices.

"It was our end of school party," I begin. "We got one of those super humid days where the temperature was about a gazillion degrees. You went to school with ghoul teachers, right?"

"You know it." After stuffing his mouth with five baby hotdogs at once, Herbie then he leans back in his chair. I take this as a good sign. The guy's getting comfortable.

"Well," I continue. "There were a lot of games, most of which sucked. But one was Dunk The Ghoul Teacher. You know the one? The teacher sits on a ledge-y thing over a pool. If you hit a bull's-eye, they fall in."

Herbie rolls his eyes. "Like anyone would do that to a ghoul. Everyone was too afraid of our overlords."

"No one did." I point at my face. "Except me."

"And I believe it." Lincoln slips onto the chair beside mine. Based on the light in his mismatched eyes, he's loving this story.

"So, my eight year old self then dunked ghouls for like five hours straight. Then the school shut down the game and I realized I was super hungry. There wasn't much food left by this point, only some scraggly baby hotdogs at the bottom of a random bowl. Even worse, they'd been sitting out in the sun and were swimming in some kind of green ooze. But I was super-hungry so I ate them all. Then I puked my guts up."

Herbie stops chewing. "Should we end this? You hate baby hotdogs. I'm part gluttony demon. I can't focus unless I'm eating. I have a doctor's note and everything."

"No, it's fine." I lie. "I just got a little shocked when I first walked in. Now I'm great."

"Really?" asks Herbie.

I rub my tummy and fake it. "Mmmm, baby hotdogs."

Herbie offers me the bowl. "Want some?"

I tap my chin, as if considering this instead of trying not to barf. "Nope, I'm good." I turn to my guy. "Lincoln, how about you?"

"I ate before we get here," says Lincoln smoothly. "Maybe next time."

"You're loss," says Herbie.

I rub my palms together. With the greetings over, it's time to focus on getting Aldred incarcerated. "Let's get to the reason we're here." Hoisting my super-sweet leather satchel, I set it onto the patch of tabletop not covered in baby hotdog bowls.

Lincoln raises his pointer finger. "Before we do that, may I ask a question?"

Herbie talks through a mouth of *yuck*. "Sure."

Lincoln tilts his head. "Not sure how to ask this, but shouldn't gluttony demons be…" he scans the room, as if looking for the word.

"A lot bigger than me?" suggests Herbie.

"That," confirms Lincoln.

"Gluttony is just about major intake of food," explains Herbie. "I've got an amazing metabolism."

"What kind of tail are you packing?" I ask.

"Hummingbird." Herbie stands up and turns around. Sure enough, he has a cute little tail of green feathers sticking out the back of his jeans. "Hummingbirds eat their weight in insects every day. For me, it's baby hotdogs."

"Your weight every day," says Lincoln. "Thank you for explaining."

Things are veering back into scary baby hotdog territory, so I decide to get us back on track. Reaching into my satchel, I pull out a leather book. "This is a codex. It's why we're here."

Slam!

The door bursts open.

I groan. Now what?

CHAPTER 3

 issy rushes into the room. Her blonde ringlets are a mess and her lips look like she just got lip fillers. No question what that means. My bestie and Zeke have been all kinds of busy. In an act of kindness from the universe, there are no spit strings dribbling from her chin.

And no, I'm not kidding. It's happened before.

"So sorry I'm late," says my bestie.

"It's fine." I wave her off. "We met Herbie and we're ready to roll. No need to stay if you're busy."

Cissy plunks herself down onto the empty seat to my right. "I'm not going anywhere. This is so important." While fanning herself with her hands, my bestie turns to Herbie. "Normally, I'm very good at hiding my emotions, but you'll just have to excuse me."

Whatever concerns Herbie had before, he's definitely moved on from them. Cissy's worry doesn't even seem to register with the kid. Herbie just stacks his latest (and now empty) bowl onto the floor, yanks over another container, and chows down.

"You see," says Cissy. "It's really-really-really important that you're here today. Myla is my best friend."

"Who?" asks Herbie.

"She means *the Great Scala* is her best friend," I say. Clearly, Herbie's not great with memory, unless it involves lunch. Goes with the hummingbird-and-gluttony combo.

"Right." Cissy exhales a long breath. "So this is super hard for me. She and her fiancée are here to gather information about Lady Adair and the House of Acca."

All the color drains from Herbie's face. "Lady Adair is dead, right? She's not doing diplomatic stuff anymore." The hummingbird side of Herbie's personality must be taking over, because the kid starts talking super fast. "I'm not Adair's intern anymore. I don't have anything to do with that crazy lady."

My brows lift. For a while, Adair acted as Antrum's diplomat to Purgatory. Seems like Herbie has quite the experience her Adair's diplomatic. Whenever we get to the evidence portion of the day, things are sure to get interesting.

"It's all right," says Lincoln soothingly. And he has that Princely way of saying things like that where you totally believe him. "Adair is gone."

"Gone where?" asks Herbie. He's wobbling a bit in his chair now. I wonder if the guy's about to pass out. That could get ugly. I decide to step in. I've dealt with guys like Herbie before. It's best to be super clear. "Lady Adair is dead. Lincoln and I totally chopped her head off."

Herbie sighs. "Good. Right. So what do you need me for again?"

And so we return to the downside of a hummingbird profile. Amazing metabolism. Short memory span.

"Adair's comes from this clan called Acca," says Cissy. "Their leader, Aldred, wants to kill Myla and Lincoln. I mean, the Great Scala and Prince Lincoln."

"Truth," I say.

Cissy sets her hand on my shoulder. "My best friend wants to take Aldred to court and make him pay for his crimes. To do this, she needs magically recorded evidence in this book." To emphasize the point, Cissy then pats the top of the leather volume with her free hand.

Lincoln and I share a pleased look. The acknowledgement is there, if unspoken. *Cissy is handling this super well.*

"And if the evidence isn't enough to win the day in court?" asks Cissy. "Then Myla and Lincoln will be locked up in a jail forever. They'll be underground with worms and nasty stuff, never to see the light of day again. I'll lose my best friend." Cissy turns to me, tears streaming down her face. "I can't lose you, Myla."

Herbie frowns. "Myla?"

Damn, this guy has a short memory.

Lincoln and I speak in unison. "Great Scala."

I press my lips together hard. Cissy is going off the rails, big time. Lincoln and I share another look. My guy angles his head toward the door. The implication is clear. *You want Cissy out of here?*

I nod quickly. *Yes, yes, yes.*

Unlike me, Lincoln is a smooth liar. He cups his hand by his ear. "Oh, my goodness. Is that Zeke?"

Cissy sniffles. "I don't hear anything."

I decide to play along. "Oh, his voice is totally clear. Zeke says he has another suit of armor to show you."

"Really?" She dabs her cheeks with her fingertips.

Lincoln fixes her with his most believable and regal stare. "Absolutely. You better hurry. I think I heard a female voice down there. Someone named Paula?"

For the record, this is super impressive. Paula Richards is Cissy's old envy nemesis from high school.

Even worse, Paula used to date Zeke. I mentioned that fact to Lincoln like once three weeks ago.

Cissy hops up to stand. Her eyes flare envy red. "Okay, you seem fine. I'll take off now."

I twiddle my fingers at her. "Buh-bye."

Cissy rushes from the room. Once the door is shut, Lincoln places a strip of purple tape on the handle. That's no ordinary cellophane. It's a magical charm from Striga. I've seen Lincoln use this particular item before. It's a locking ward, so no one can disturb us again. Nice idea.

Key fact: Herbie is so into his baby hotdogs, the kid doesn't even notice Lincoln setting up the charm.

My guy retakes his seat and turns to me. "Shall we?"

"Absolutely." I refocus on Herbie. "Are you ready to tell your story?"

"Adair's dead right?"

"Totally."

Herbie shoves a fresh handful of baby hotdogs into his mouth. "Then, lets do this."

I grin. *Let's do this indeed.* Once we lock in this evidence, we're one step closer to taking Acca down.

About time.

CHAPTER 4

At last, we're about to lock in our first anti-Acca interview. Squirming in my chair, I try to focus on a single thought.

Do not look at the baby hotdogs.

Do not look at the baby hotdogs.

Do not look at the baby hotdogs.

Crap, I looked. *Whoa, that kid can pack in the grub.* Honestly. We haven't been here that long and already, Herbie's halfway through the bowls.

Note to self: thank Cissy later for rounding up so much food. Because once these containers are empty? Herbie will be gone so fast, little poofs of smoke will appear behind him as he runs.

"Let's start with the basics," says Lincoln. "The

process of recording your testimony is unique to my people."

"What do you mean?" For someone with a mouthful of food, Herbie speaks pretty clearly. Guess he has a lot of practice. "I watch Mortal's Court. People give testimony all the time."

Yet again, my many hours of television watching prove crucial to my adult life. "It's like this," I say to Herbie. "When humans have a trial, witnesses take the stand in court. In Antrum, you must be thrax to enter the courtroom." Or in my case, a demigoddess who hates rules. But I won't go into that much detail with Herbie. After all, the guy has a hummingbird attention span. "So for your testimony to count, it must be recorded in this particular book." I gesture to the leather volume. "The Rixa Codex."

"So you write what I say in the book?" asks Herbie.

"No, the process involves magic," explains Lincoln. "But it will not affect your person. Is that acceptable?"

Herbie grips his current bowl, dragging it across the table with long screech. "What about my food?"

"The magic won't affect it," clarifies Lincoln.

Herbie shrugs. "In that case, we're good." In a surprise move, Herbie then goes back to eating.

Lincoln lifts the codex. "I, Lincoln Vidar Osric Aquilus from the House of Rixa—"

"Hold on," says Herbie. "That's a lot of names for just one guy. Is this another thrax thing?"

A heavy pause fills the air. My eyes widen. *That's right.* I only introduced Lincoln as my fiancée, and my guy's not in formalwear today. I wince, debating whether to tell Herbie everything. Trouble is, this kid seems easily derailed.

Evidently, Lincoln has the same idea.

"That's exactly what it is," says my guy. "A thrax thing." Stretching out his arms, Lincoln balances the codex on his palms. "Let the recording begin." The codex rises from Lincoln's hands and then hovers in the center of the room. A flare of white light pulses across its cover.

Herbie stops eating for a whole hot second. "Cool."

"First question," I say. "How did you become Adair's intern?"

"It's like this," says Herbie. "I eat a ton of Happy Piggy baby hotdogs. Those are gourmet. Really expensive. I needed summer job to help pay my bills. The rest of the internships here paid next to nothing. Working with angels was the worst. Only minimum wage."

I nod. *That makes sense. Angels can be cheap sometimes.*

"But interning for the Thrax Diplomat paid major money. I guess Adair went through twelve interns, and every time one left, they upped the salary. So I applied for the job. Sure, I heard she was a little loco. Still, I thought that as long as I got my Happy Piggies, everything would be fine."

"Let me guess," I state. "There was a reason it paid so well."

"You got that right," says Herbie. "All Adair did was yell at me. I couldn't do anything right. She kept saying how I'm a demon so her family would kill me for screwing things up so much. Which is really anti-quasi." Herbie rolls his eyes. "We are not demons. Quasis mostly human with a tiny bit of demonic DNA."

I raise my hand. "Testify." Leaning forward, I rest my chin on my palms. *Things are getting interesting.* "So what kind of work did she have you do?"

Herbie runs his tongue over his teeth for a moment. I think the move helps him think while simultaneously picking bits of hotdog off his gums. "Adair took milk baths in the morning, and I had to fill the tub. That took tons of my time every day."

My mouth falls open. "She what?"

"Made me get a ton of milk cartons and pour it into a bathtub," sys Herbie.

"No way." I'm having trouble with this concept for some reason. *I mean, milk baths? Who does that?*

"Oh, yeah. There's a diplomatic suite in the mansion. Comes complete with a tub and everything. I had to clean up after she was done." Herbie sticks out his tongue in the universal gag-face. "Never drinking milk again, I'll tell you that."

"I don't blame you." Purgatory milk tends to curdle fast. That cleanup must have been a bitch.

"And what else did you do for Adair?" asks Lincoln.

That's my guy, moving things on from the milk conversation. Clever.

"Adair had me tie her shoes. I made sure her office was filled with fresh flowers every morning. She wanted crystals put all over the place too. Oh, and every day I got her really specific lunches that she never ate. And no matter what I did, she screamed at me for screwing it up. Those death threats from her family." Herbie shivers. "Working for her was terrible. I stopped eating. Sleeping. My hair started falling out."

"So you were a diplomatic intern who did nothing related to diplomacy," I recap.

"That's it." Herbie eats another handful, his eyes lost in thought. After a pause, he snaps his fingers. The movement sends a shower of hotdog juice over the table. "Oh, yeah. I almost forgot. Adair would talk at me all the time. The other interns, too. I mean, if she caught you by the snack machine, she'd talk your head off."

"About diplomatic stuff?" I ask.

"No. About how she really wanted to marry her

Angelbound love. Yakkity yakkity yakkity. Non stop. *Angelbound love, Angelbound love, Angelbound love.* All the interns called him the *Miserybound loser.*"

There's a long moment where the words hang out there.

Miserybound loser.

Oh, this is too good.

I pretend to cough, but the sound comes out sounding a lot like, *told you so.* I still give Lincoln crap about even considering marriage to Adair. Talk about a horror show.

Lincoln gives me the side-eye while smoothing his brow with his middle finger. *Classic.*

"Back to Adair," says my guy smoothly. "Did she say anything about unsanctioned alliances with Hell?"

"Oh sure. She said she was sharing blood with the King of Hell. Armageddon. He was going to possess her and in exchange, she'd be able to steal the powers of the Great Scala and marry her Miserybound loser." Herbie makes little air quotes with his fingers when he says Miserybound loser.

"Unholy Hell." I gasp, because this news is just so crazy pants. "Did you tell anyone?"

"Why would I?" asks Herbie. "Who would believe that someone was crazy enough to share blood with the King of Hell? I just thought it was Adair being Adair."

"And did Adair say who set up this deal with Armageddon?"

"Sure," replies Herbie. "It was all brokered by Adair's own father, the Earl of Acca. Or so she said. Like I told you before, it was just so nutty it couldn't be true. Was it?"

I hold my thumb and pointer finger an inch apart. "It was a little true."

"Whoa." This time, Herbie jams so many baby hotdogs in his mouth, he actually has trouble speaking. "Wath happenth?"

"The dead thing," I reply. "But back to Adair. Anything else about her and Hell that you want to share?"

"Mmm," Herbie finally chews and swallows his bite-a-saurus. "Adair talked all the time about how she was close to Armageddon. That if she ever went to Hell, the place would be a vacation for her. I thought for sure it was a joke."

"It wasn't," I say. "Long story."

Lincoln then launches into a ton more questions about Adair, Armageddon and Aldred. My guy's able to get some more details out, but there are no more major revelations like the whole Miserybound loser thing. Eventually, it gets really clear that we're out of useful queries.

"That's all we require from you," says Lincoln.

"Are you sure?" asks Herbie. "I can give you more details on the bath-thing."

"Nope, we're good," I say. I really don't want to know more about Adair's bathing habits.

"Whatever you say." Reaching over, Herbie drags the final bowl in front of him. Wow. How did the guy eat so quickly?

Oh, right. Gluttony demon.

"One last thing," says Herbie. "This Miserybound loser guy, do you know him?"

Lincoln nods. "I do."

"Pass along a message for me. Adair said that if the Miserybound loser ever married someone else, she'd find a way to drag him to Hell and make his after-life terrible. Same thing with her father. If Miserybound loser married not-Adair, then Aldred had plans for the guy, too. Adair wouldn't say what the schemes were, but the way her eyes got all glazed over with a sick kind of happy? It wasn't good."

"I'll pass it along," says Lincoln. "Although I don't think he'll be concerned."

Now Lincoln may not care about that news, but my insides twist with worry.

"In my opinion," continues Herbie. "That Misery-bound loser guy should never walk down the aisle. Total disaster." Herbie looks down at his bowl. Somewhere along the line, he finished off his last baby hotdog. "I'm empty." His eyes bulge. "I'm empty!" Rising, he rushes from the room.

For a moment, I consider following him. After all, Herbie just helped us out. I want to make sure the kid is okay. That said, the Herbie's been dealing with his gluttony side for years. No doubt, he has a stash of baby hotdogs somewhere. And there are more important concerns.

Like what Herbie said about Adair and marriage.

Are Lincoln and I making a mistake?

CHAPTER 5

Even with Herbie gone, all this talk about my marriage and Acca-related doom keeps buzzing around my head. Not to mention the part about Adair vacationing in Hell? Seems totally fake.

I turn to Lincoln. "Adair in Hell … does that worry you at all?"

"Not in particular. In fact, I just got some news on that topic this morning. Would you like to hear it?"

We'd been concerned about Adair ever since she chose yelling at Lincoln and me over going to Heaven. Lincoln knows some fallen angels in Hell. My guy reached out for information. Tilting my head, I consider whether or not I want the update. It's already been a lot of Adair this morning. In the end, I decide it's best to get it over with.

"Sure," I reply.

"As it turns out, Adair's relatively comfortable for now. I wouldn't call her stay in Hell a vacation, but Armageddon is protecting her from the worst. The King of Hell wants to keep making deals with Acca. Torturing the Earl's favorite daughter won't necessarily help in that regard."

I think this through. "But once the Earl is dead, things could change for Adair. Eternity is a looooong time."

"Correct. Yet she made her choices. Just as we're making ours."

A weight of worry settles onto my shoulders. I curl forward, resting my elbows on the table before me. "Maybe this is a bad idea. Going after Acca. Getting married."

Lincoln's face turns unreadable. Amazing how he can do that in a second flat. "Because your feelings for me have changed?" he asks.

"Never." I huff out a breath. "It's Aldred. He'll never give up."

Lincoln shifts in his chair, moving to face me. Little by little, he takes my hands in his. The movement makes me turn to face him straight on. My guy meets my gaze straight on before speaking once more. "I have a duty to my people. It will be performed better with you at my side. But I also have an obligation to myself. To us. My father lives in fear of Aldred. I won't do that. More than anything, I want a future with you."

What sweet words. I should feel all better now. Yet I don't. If anything, my weight of worry only seems to grow heavier. "But you know Aldred will scheme about our wedding. Herbie is right. It could be a disaster."

"Whatever happens, we'll face it together. That's what this is about, isn't it?"

In this moment, Lincoln is all princely determination. Some of my anxiety fades. My guy and I have faced down a ton of stuff. Maybe we can ace this as well.

"Be my wife, Myla." Leaning in, Lincoln brushes the gentlest of kisses across my lips. The sensation makes my insides turn all warm and lovey. "Say yes. Again."

And because Lincoln's not the only one who wants this more than anything, I reply with one word. "Yes."

—The End—

The adventure continues in our fourth story, Savings Mrs. Pomplemousse!

FIVE. SAVING MRS. POMPLEMOUSSE

Introduction From the Author, Christina Bauer

Dear reader,

This story takes place *after* the events of *Acca*, which is the third book in the Angelbound Origins series. Having finished up her wedding adventures, Myla visits Mrs. Pomplemousse, an elderly quasi lady who helped Myla and Lincoln.

I hope you enjoy *Saving Mrs. Pomplemousse!*

Sincerely,

CB

Saving Mrs.
Pomplemousse

lmost there.

I jog along a concrete sidewalk in one of Purgatory's swankier neighborhoods. *East Malacoda.* A light drizzle falls. The smell of freshly-cut grass fills the air. Row houses flank either side of the street—their brick facades buckle with age. I scan the building numbers.

Thirty-two. Getting closer.

As I rush long, I pat the front pocket of my jeans. It's the spot where I stashed the note from Mrs. Pomplemousse, aka the woman who helped me destroy the evil earl of Acca. I picture the words.

Dear Myla,

Do not worry if you hear any dark rumors about my person. I am fine. No matter what...
DO NOT VISIT MY HOUSE.

Mrs. P

I ask around. Few people even know that Mrs. P exists. No one shares any nasty rumors about her.

Which gets me thinking.

The last time I saw Mrs. P, she was acting more than a little bit odd. And now, she wants me *not* to stop by? That's the very definition of 'hidden cry for help.' I check the house numbers again.

Number Thirteen.

Finally, I'm here.

After rushing up the thin staircase, I reach the front door. My tail rings the bell.

Nothing happens.

With every passing moment, my pulse speeds a little faster.

Please, let Mrs. P be alright.

I ring the bell again. Four times. While I wait, I scan the rest of Malacoda Lane, looking for trouble. There are matching brick row houses. Lots of yellowing grass. And mucho sidewalk puddles. Everything looks fine.

At last, a jangle of keys sounds before the door opens a crack to reveal Mrs. P.

And dang, but does she look different.

It takes a moment for me to process the change. Her brown eyes remain large and expressive. Mrs. P also sports the same wisdom lines and gray hair. Only now, her hair is so white, it looks more pale blonde than anything else. And Mrs. P has swapped out her bulky tweed suit for a little black dress that shows off her curves.

All of a sudden, I feel a little underdressed. My long red hair is a frizzy mess. I wear skinny jeans and a black shirt. Meanwhile, Mrs. P looks ready for a night on the town.

"Hello," she says smoothly. "Who are you?"

As the daughter of the President of Purgatory—and the only being who can move this woman's soul to Heaven or Hell—you'd think my face would be recognizable.

Only, that isn't the big issue here. Last time I stopped by, Mrs. P spoke with an old-lady warble. Now, her voice is high-pitched and smooth.

It's like she was playing a part before. Huh.

"Don't take this the wrong way," I begin. "But is that your *real* voice?"

"Of course, it is."

"Were you in Purgatory's witness protection program, by any chance? I know you had access to ghoul records. If folks knew incriminating stuff about our old overlords then, Mom—*I mean, the President of Purgatory*—helped them hide after the ghouls took off. Was that you?"

"Absolutely not."

"Well, you've changed since the last time I saw you. Not that it's a bad thing."

Mrs. P leans in so close, she now appears as nothing but a sliver of face beyond the mostly-closed door. "I know who you are. Myla Lewis."

"That's right. I'm here to check on you."

Like all residents of Purgatory, Mrs. P and I are both quasi demons—meaning mostly human with a touch of Hellish DNA. Unlike most of our home realm, Mrs. P and I share the same demon heritage. *Furor dragon.* That gives us deadly sin powers over lust as well as wrath. It also means we sport the best kind of tail: long, dark and covered in dragonscales.

Right now, Mrs. P's tail lurks guiltily around her ankle. *Yet another warning sign.*

"Why would you do that? I asked you not to!"

"You know those videos where a hostage says their captors are super nice and you don't need to worry?"

"Sure."

"Your note was kinda like that. Plus, you were acting so strangely the last time I saw you."

Mrs. P nods slowly. "I did see you recently. Was it at an arena match?"

"Kind of. It was supposed to be a wedding." I lower my voice. "Please, tell me. Is anything wrong?"

"Nothing at all. And if I did anything odd at your wedding, it was not a sign of trouble." She forces a smile. "Now, if you'll excuse me."

Boom! Boom!

Loud thumps echo from inside Mrs. P's home. A jolt of alarm moves down my back.

"That's trouble, Mrs. P."

In reply, Mrs. P tries to shut her door in my face. *Not happening.* Before she can slam anything, my tail darts forward. The arrowhead-shaped end works like a wedge to open the door.

"Not so fast," I state. "What was that noise?"

Mrs. P blinks innocently. "What noise?"

Boom! Boom!

"That one."

"The shutter on my bedroom window is broken and flapping around." She tilts her head and smiles. "I appreciate your concern, but I'm fine, honestly."

Boom! Boom!

This time, a man's voice sounds as well. "Argh!"

Now, things are getting serious.

"Okay, enough chit chat."

I shoulder the door open and step inside.

I walk around Mrs. P's living room. Some things are similar to my last visit. There's faded green wallpaper printed with tiny flowers. The scent of old people and mothballs fills the air. Some overly pouffy furniture surrounds a small tea table.

What's different are the many stacks of leather-bound books everywhere.

"As you can see, I've brought down a few books from storage."

"I can see that." I step up to a nearby pile. A heavy book sits on top. The title catches my eye right away. *"Aquila's Adventures Through Time."* I scoop up the volume and leaf through the pages. "No copies of this are supposed to be in existence anymore."

"Correct." Mrs. P gingerly lifts the tome from my

hands and resets it on the stack. "Which is why I'd like to keep it between us."

"That was written five hundred years ago."

"What?"

My tail points at the volume. I pat the arrowhead-shaped end. "Thanks, boy." I refocus on Mrs. P. "That book. How did you get it?"

"Would you believe me if I said it came from the Earl of Acca?"

"Sure," I reply. "But would that be the truth?"

Boom! Boom!

"At last. Progress." I step around in a circle and examine the room. Small fracture lines fan out across the ceiling. I swear, they weren't so pronounced when I first entered. "That noise is coming from your attic. Care to give me a tour?"

"I'll show you," she says primly. "Just remember one thing. He won't hurt me."

I do a double-take. "He won't hurt you?"

"Yes, that's what I said. Now, follow me."

And I do follow, but I've one big question in mind.

Oh, Mrs. P. What are you up to?

I trail Mrs. P up two flights of stairs. The rest of the house looks like the living room. I'm talking about pretty wallpaper, puffy furniture and stacks of rare books. Unlike what I saw on the first floor, these volumes are all from human writers, from Shakespeare to Mary Shelley.

A rope dangles from the ceiling. Mrs. P pulls on the line. A panel breaks free above us. A set of steps descend from the ceiling. Mrs. P marches up the stairs and into the attic above. While her tail looked guilty before, now it bobs behind her in a kind of happy dance.

Whatever is in the attic, Mrs. P is definitely *not* afraid.

After marching up the stairs, I enter a dark and cramped space. Seconds pass while my eyes adjust to the dim light. The room is A-frame in terms of its build. Exposed beams angle overhead. A small cot sits in one corner. A janky air conditioner is jammed into a nearby window. And as Mrs. P stated, there is someone in the room.

Not sure who I expected, but it wasn't this.

Before me, there stands a handsome demon with a bare chest, long black hair and leather pants. Dark bat-style wings arch from his back. Horns wind up from his head. A dragonscale tail sways behind him. Only one supernatural man meets this profile. A tundran. These are male demons who live in arctic climates.

Suddenly, the whole *Mrs. P makeover situation* makes a lot more sense.

YVES

The tundran marches across the floor. Every step reverberates through the house.

Boom! Boom!

He pauses before the air conditioner and fiddles with the levers and dials. Even from here, I can tell he's not making any progress. The tundran grumbles under his breath. But demons being supernatural, the noise echoes through the room.

"Argh!"

Poor guy. Tundrans run hot, so they love to hang out in snowy landscapes without shirts. Many take up with polar bear families.

True fact. Unless you're a baby seal, tundrans are pretty harmless.

And Mrs. P has one her attic. In fact, the place is

done up as a nice little apartment, so long as you don't count the broken air conditioner. He's living here.

I mean, Mrs. P is part lust demon like me, so I cognitively understand why she would want a handsome roomie. But a tundran demon would rather have his wings clipped than live indoors.

The tundran looks to Mrs. P. "Aren't introductions in order, cherie?" He has a cute French accent because, of course, he does.

"Oh, yes." Mrs. P gestures between me and the demon. "Myla, Yves. Yves, Myla."

Yves shoots Mrs. P a panty-melting grin. "Nothing else to say, mon coeur?"

"He's my…" Mrs. P twists her hands at her waistline. "It's complicated." She rounds on me. "As you can see, I'm perfectly fine. Don't you want to leave now?"

"Au contraire," intones Yves. "I'd rather if Myla stayed for a bit."

I nod. "Oh, I'm staying alright."

"That is completely unacceptable. You must leave." She turns to Yves. "And you can't stay, either. Both of you, Out!"

Yves leans against the wall. "I haven't seen you this upset since the Library of Alexandria burned. But then, you raced through the flames to save… what was it again?"

"The collected poetry of Sappo." Mrs. P lifts her chin. "Anyone would have done that."

"You were alive in ancient Egypt?" I ask.

Mrs. P shrugs. "Yes."

"How does that work, exactly?

"I was cursed many years ago," begins Mrs. P.

"I'd call it a blessing," counters Yves.

"I get reincarnated over and over. Around age seventeen, I remember Yves and our history.

"Then, she runs." Yves grins. "And you know how it is with predators. We love it when you run."

"I do it for a reason." Mrs. P hugs her elbows. "Because I die over and over. You don't. And every time you lose me, it makes life miserable for you."

"But every time you run, it makes me so very happy again." Yves looks to me. "This escape is one of her best. My Anaïs has never been born a quasi demon before. And taking on a married name. That is new as well."

"It's a fake name," says the woman who's real name is Anaïs.

"It threw me off." Yves shrugs. "It took extra time to find you." He looks to me. "She really thought I'd given up. And ever since I reappeared, she's been a bit muddled. Doing all sorts of odd things one minute, then forgetting about them the next second."

I bob my head and consider. "That explains how Mrs. P—*I mean, Anaïs*—acted at my wedding."

Anaïs pales. "You got married? When?"

"You know what? Never mind." I focus on Anaïs. "What's the problem here, really?"

"I'm old and ugly now."

"And I'm not leaving," says Yves.

"I'm just going to die on your again and break your heart."

"My heart to break."

Anaïs rounds on me again. "Look at me. Look at him. We can't be soul mates. Tell him."

I throw up my hands. "Hey, I'm with Yves. I never buy it when someone decides that a supermodel is their soul mates. You and him being connected through time? Now that, I believe."

Yves bows his head. "Thank you."

"De nada."

He stalks closer to Anaïs. "We have been together through many forms and lives. Talk to me Anaïs. You'll remember our connection."

"No, this must end. Find someone else."

"Then it seems we are at an impasse, cherie."

One of my favorite pastimes is impromptu battle strategy. This conversation between Yves and Anaïs doesn't involve swords, but it's a fight all the same. My mind spins through all the books I saw on the way up here… Yves story about the Library of Alexandria… and the fact that Anaïs won't talk to Yves about anything but him leaving.

I raise my hand. "I may be able to help here."

Anaïs turns to me. "How?"

"My mother is President of Purgatory. I'm the Great Scala. Whether with a deportation order or a supernatural igni ride to someplace that's not here… I can make Yves depart."

Anaïs sighs. "And you'll do that?"

"Yves must ask you three questions about any topic I choose. If you still wish him to go, then he has to leave." I look to the tundran. "What do you say?"

"I agree."

"As do I," adds Anaïs.

"Let's do this thing." I rub my palms together.

Here comes the good stuff.

"Let the games begin." I focus on Yves. "You may now ask Anaïs three questions about authors."

"Bien sur. Anaïs, what did you think of Jane Austen?"

"Great author." Anaïs curls her mouth in vague disgust. "Only, she tended to spit when speaking."

Now, I cognitively realize that Anaïs and Yves have been running around for a long time. Still, this little tidbit is a shocker.

"You knew Jane Austen?" I ask.

"Yes," replies Anaïs. "She's lovely. A spitter, but lovely. Second question."

"Two,' Declares Yves. "What do you think of the Bronte sisters?"

"Charming. Strong writers. Emily did the right thing to drop that silly affair in France."

After years in the arena, I can sense when a warrior is going in for the kill. And based on the gleam in Yves's eyes? That's exactly what he's about to do now.

"What about..." Yves rocks on his heels. "Say, Ayn Rand?"

Anaïs narrows her eyes. "Don't get me started!"

Yves blinks innocently. "You did not enjoy her book, *Atlas Shrugged?*"

"Bah! It should have been called *Atlas Whined.*" Anaïs turns to me. "Spoiler alert. are you sure you want to hear this?"

"I'm good."

"Because this is a book you'll have strong emotions about. I don't want to ruin the experience for you."

"I have a long list of books to tackle." I count them off on my fingers. "*Demonpedia... DIY Weapons, Volume Eight... Chicken Soup For Your Tail.* I've a very busy reading schedule. I can honestly say I will never get to *Atlas Shrugged.*"

My tail pops up. The arrowed-head-shaped end is angled for a particular motion. I give it a high five. "That chicken soup is coming, bud."

"If you insist," says Anaïs. "*Atlas Shrugged* is a book

about all the smarty pants people leaving society to hang out in a hidden valley together. They expect the rest of the world to collapse without their magnificence."

"Huh. That's odd."

"It's beyond odd. It's irrational. Who'll do the dishes and scrub the toilets in this intellectual Valhalla? Don't you understand?"

Let the record show, I do understand this. But for reasons of true love, I decide to play dumb.

"Nope. I still don't get it."

"Sometimes," adds Anaïs. "We forget about those sometimes-silent people in our lives who make life possible." When she looks over to her tundran. "Like you."

The tundran speeds across the room to scoop Anaïs in his arms. She smiles so broadly, I see the beautiful young woman was before and is now. While they have their moment, I tiptoe out of the attic and take off.

I don't want to be like, la la la, I'm so awesome, but…

La. Le. La. La. I am so awesome.

And although I stepped into this house with a mindful of worry, I leave with a far different thought.

You go, Anaïs and Yves.

~

—The End—

The adventure continues in Angelbound Tales, Volume Two!

Revisit ANGELBOUND, the kick-ass paranormal romance with more than 1 million copies sold!

OFFSPRING

The next generation takes on Heaven, Hell, and everything in MAXON, Book 1 of Angelbound Offspring!

• SPECIAL EXTENDED EDITION •
ANGELBOUND
MAXON
NEW EPILOGUE INCLUDED
BOOK ONE OF THE OFFSPRING SERIES
CHRISTINA BAUER

FAIRY TALES OF THE MAGICORUM

A modern fairy tale that *USA Today* calls a 'must-read!' Check out WOLVES AND ROSES!

BEHOLDER

Medieval mages ... Slow-burn love ... And heart-pounding action! Check out the BEHOLDER series!

PIXIELAND DIARIES tells the story of sassy pixie Calla and 'her' elf prince, Dare.

APPENDIX

Angelbound Origins

About a quasi (part demon and part human) girl who loves kicking butt in Purgatory's Arena

1. Angelbound
2. Scala
3. Acca
4. Thrax
5. The Dark Lands
6. The Brutal Time
7. Armageddon
8. Quasi Redux
9. Clockwork Igni
10. Lady Reaper
11. Reaper Wars
12. Angry Gods

Angelbound Lincoln

The Angelbound experience as told by Prince Lincoln

1. Duty Bound
2. Lincoln
3. Trickster
4. Baculum
5. Angelfire

Angelbound Offspring

The next generation takes on Heaven, Hell, and every-thing in between

1. Maxon
2. Portia
3. Zinnia
4. Rhodes
5. Kaps
6. Mack
7. Huntress

Angelbound Xavier

1. Archenemy
2. Archnemesis
3. Archangel

Fairy Tales of the Magicorum

Modern fairy tales with sass, action, and romance

1. Wolves and Roses

2. Moonlight and Midtown

3. Shifters and Glyphs

4. Slippers and Thieves

5. Bandits and Ball Gowns

6. Fire and Cinder

7. Fairies and Frosting

8. Towers and Tithes

9. Mirrors and Mysteries

10. Rapunzels and Powers

Dimension Drift

Dystopian adventures with science, snark, and hot aliens

1. Scythe

2. Umbra

3. Alien Minds

4. ECHO Academy

** This is a finished series.*

Pixieland Diaries

About sassy pixie Calla and her love-crush-nemesis, the elf prince Dare

1. Pixieland Diaries

2. Calla

3. Dare

** This is a finished series.*

Beholder

Where a medieval farm girl discovers necromancy and true love

1. Cursed
2. Concealed
3. Cherished
4. Crowned
5. Cradled

**This is a finished series.*

...Please consider leaving a review, even if it's just a line or two. Every bit truly helps, especially for those of us who don't *write by the numbers,* if you know what I mean.

Plus I have it on good authority that every time you review an indie author, somewhere an angel gets a mocha latte. For reals.

And angels need their caffeine, too.

ACKNOWLEDGMENTS

If you're reading my freaking acknowledgements, chances are, I should thank you for something. So, for the record: you are awesome, dear reader.

That said, huge and heartfelt thanks must go out to my husband and son for their rock-solid support. Being an author means a lot of early mornings, late nights, long weekends, and never-ending patience. You two are the best guys in the universe, period.

After that, I must thank the extensive network of reviewers, friends and colleagues who helped me build my writing chops in general. Gracias.

Finally, deep affection goes out to my late, much loved, and dearly missed Aunt Sandy and Uncle Henry. You saw the writer in me, always. Thank you, first and last.

Christina Bauer thinks that fantasy books are like bacon: they just make life better. All of which is why she writes romance novels that feature demons, dragons, wizards, witches, elves, elementals, and a bunch of random stuff that she brainstorms while riding the Boston T. Oh, and she includes lots of humor and kick-ass chicks, too. Christina lives in Newton, MA with her husband, son, and semi-insane golden retriever, Ruby.

Stalk Christina on Social Media

Blog:
http://monsterhousebooks.com/blog/category/ christina

Facebook:
https://www.facebook.com/authorBauer/

Instagram:
https://www.instagram.com/christina_cb_bauer/

Twitter:
@CB_Bauer

VLOG:
https://tinyurl.com/Vlogbauer

Web site:
www.bauersbooks.com